Ten Minute Warning

Em Dehaney

Copyright © Em Dehaney

ISBN- 9798646373251
Cover artwork by Matthew Cash

Also by Em Dehaney

Food of The Gods

The Wassailers

After Us

The Searcher of The Thames

INTRODUCTION

Welcome to Ten Minute Warning, my second short fiction collection. Enter freely of your own will, and leave some of the happiness you bring.

Thank you, as always, to Matty-Bob Cash, my partner in grime at Burdizzo Books, and to our whole extended Burdizzo Family including, but not exclusively, Jonathan Butcher, David and Tara Court, The Evil Claw himself Christopher Law, The Queen Of Filth Dani Brown, Peter Germany, Paul B. Morris, Pardip Basra, Paula D. Ashe, Jessica McHugh, Sam Jewiss, Paul Hisock, Lex H. Jones, Rebecca Lambert, The Raven Twins Cat and Lynx, The Might DLD, Duncan Bradshaw, Linda Nagle, Richard Wall, Priya Sharma and Matt Hill. Huge apologies to anyone I have forgotten.

Thank you to all my friends and family who have supported me and my writing, especially everyone who came to The Three Daws for the launch party for my novel The Searcher Of The Thames, and witnessed the haunted pub for themselves during my reading.

For those who like to jump straight into the stories themselves, take yourself off to page 13, do not pass Go, do not collect £200.

For those who like to know more about the inspiration behind my stories, read on (you also do not collect £200, sorry).

Caravan of Love was first published in The Burdizzo Mix-Tape Vol 1 in 2019, a collection of stories inspired by Matty-Bob and my favourite songs. I chose Caravan of Love by The Housemartins, a favourite of Matty's, but also a song from my childhood.

Five Gold Rings was taken from the second Burdizzo Christmas anthology; 12 Days 2017. There is nothing remotely Christmassy about this story.

Ten Minute Warning was first printed in Burdizzo Books Visions From The Void in 2018. This project was the brainchild of Jonathan Butcher, and every story was inspired by a piece of op-art created by his father, Les. My image looked like an apocalyptic explosion, a nuclear mushroom cloud as seen from above. North Korea were deep in their warhead testing cycle and the news story about the false nuclear warning in Hawaii had recently been on the TV, so I started to think about what might happen if you were trapped in a makeshift bunker with your family, not knowing what was happening in the outside world. How grimly ironic that just 18 months or so after this story was published, the Covid-19 lockdown came into force and we all got to experience the reality of being locked inside with just our immediate family for company (or if we lived alone, no company at all) for months on end.

The Rape Of Ivy House was originally published in Sparks: An Electric Anthology, another Burdizzo release. It was the first "ghost story" I ever wrote, and was described by a reviewer as being like a classic episode of Tales Of The Unexpected, which made me a rather happy writer.

The Tiger & The Lamb was written during the Covid-19 lockdown, but came from a collection of loose ideas I had well over a year before. The first part of the puzzle was the song Best Finest Surgeon by St Vincent, which I learned was inspired by the diaries of Marilyn Monroe. Reading up on Monroe, the more I learned, the angrier I got that she is viewed purely as a tragic sex-symbol. As with many women in the public eye who died young (Diana Spencer, Amy Winehouse, Caroline Flack) her looks, her weight, her physical and mental health, her substance abuse, her sex life, everything about her was picked and prodded over by the media, so that even the reporting of her death was just another scandal to sell papers. This in turn takes us to the next part of the puzzle – The Black Dahlia Murder. As a Jack The Ripper obsessive, The Black Dahlia Murder holds similar fascination, with added Hollywood glamour.

The salacious way the press reported the murder of Elizabeth Short, and the amount of false stories that circulated (and continue to circulate) about her sexuality, about her deformed genitalia, about her loose morals, I began to see Elizabeth and Marilyn as kindred spirits; The Black Dahlia and The White Rose, both victims of Hollywood in different ways.

Herring Girl was a bespoke story written for the wonderful Tara Court, as a prize for winning the 2019 Burdizzo Halloween Costume Competition. Tara very kindly allowed her story to be included here.

Hannah's Story was the original prologue to my novel The Searcher Of The Thames, and some of you may recognise elements that I wove into the story (a LOT of darlings were killed in the making of that book!). I feel like it still deserves to stand on its own two feet.

Little Miss Colorado Dream Queen was first published in Welcome To A Town Called Hell in 2018. This was a collaborative novel set in a Colorado town just after a devastating plane crash opens up a portal to Hell. It was originally dreamed up by Calum Chalmers, but for various reasons he was unable to see the project through to the end, so he entrusted his baby to Matty-Bob and myself. I hope we did you proud Calum.

The idea for Elvers came around the same time as my Marilyn Monroe obsession. I even did a Twitter poll to see which I should write first. The public spoke, and I wrote this "eels and moon goddesses" story in the summer of 2019.

As with my first collection, Food Of The Gods, I like to finish up with a poem. Fire Escape was first published in Within Darkness & Light, from Paul B. Morris's Nothing Books in 2017. It was inspired by a very dear friend of mine who suffers with a condition called Chronic Regional Pain Syndrome. And yes, it is as horrible as it sounds.

This book contains ten tales of darkness and horror, in all its many forms.

You have been warned.

Em Dehaney, July 2020

CARAVAN OF LOVE

He pushes his thumb and forefinger, cracked and calloused from years of turpentine and splinters, against the handle of his chisel, driving the blade across the surface of the wood. He trusts the sycamore. Can feel its every bend and groove, knew when it would warp, when it would break. His hands, so deft and sure despite their looks, caress the wood. He runs his little finger with the lightest touch along the ridge he has just carved. It was smooth, with not a snag or jagged edge.

He kept his tools sharp.

Gripping the chisel firmly, he took the point back to the start, carving another line which swooped alongside the first. A delicate curl of wood formed under the blade, like a snail shell.

Carve. Swoop. Curl.

Carve. Swoop. Curl.

Carve. Swoop. Curl.

Soon, the form of a bird began to rise from the timber. Then another. A pair of turtle doves, feathering their nest. He always painted his motifs in pairs, using his own blend of linseed oil and powdered oxide, fiercely guarding his secret recipe from the other waggon builders.

He knew all about keeping secrets.

Contrary to what most non-Gypsies, or *gorjas*, believe, the building and decorating of waggons was one of a few talents the travelling folk looked for outside their own tight-knit communities. The *vardos* were not just their homes and modes of transport, but symbols of wealth and status. A life on the road did not allow for many possessions, particularly those that did not serve any practical purpose. So the practical became the beautiful, and they paid men like my father to carve and paint ornate patterns on the bodies of their trailers. This soon became a competition between families, and at the summer fairs they would show off the gold-leaf, the intricate lining-out in grassy greens, buttercup yellows and chalky whites, and the bunches of wooden grapes that looked so shiny and juicy, like you could pluck one off and pop it in your mouth.

I remember the first time my Pa took me to Appleby horse fair. It was like landing on an alien world or in some exotic, far-flung country. I was surrounded by men shouting in fast tongues I did not understand, by bartering and hurly-burly. Dark-eyed women stared out from trailers. Shirtless boys, younger than I was, rode huge ponies, driving them to wash in the river. I dodged steaming piles of horse dung and dogs and small children. The smell of cooking mingled with the sweat of men and ponies made me light headed. Pa set up his trailer, gaily painted with the words Collins and Son.

Then he took me to my first bare-knuckle fight.

'Don't tell your Ma,' he said, handing over a few coins to a round man with a book and pencil. 'If you come to a fight and don't put a wager on, you're nothing more than a ghoul.'

I had no money, could make no bet, but I knew I was no ghoul the moment I heard the first crack of knuckle on jaw. The scarlet arc as teeth connected with bone and the spray of blood that splattered my boots. I pushed my way through the crowd, back into the thick wood smoke and meaty mist of the camps. That was when I first saw her. Just a kid, like me. Her face lit from below, those heavy, serious brows and blue eyes that danced above the firelight. She held up a morsel of food in her hand, without smiling, but still in a gesture of welcome. I ambled over and she passed me a tiny leg of hare. I could taste the grass under its feet as it coursed through the meadow. I could taste the sunlight on its ears and the rain of a spring shower dripping from its waxy fur.

'Your first fair.'

It wasn't a question.

'Yes. How did you know?'

'You got the look, is all, got the smell.'

'You're going to talk to me about smells? How can you smell anything other than horse shit?'

This made her laugh.

'*Gorja* boy. You live brick, you don't know The Way.'

'What's your name?'

'Elvie.'

'I'm Jack. Jack Collins.'

'I know,' she said, pointing to the side of my Pa's waggon.

'Have you been to Appleby before?'

'I was born here, *gorja* boy. In that waggon, right there.'

We talked for a while, warmed by the fire. I had a hundred questions for her, but soon my Pa came running along the muddy path. As he got closer, I could see his cheek starting to swell up and grazes on the backs of his hands.

'It turned into a brawl, Jack. Bloody great brawl, everyone swinging punches and hooting and yelling.'

He didn't look frightened though, he looked alive. His good eye glinting and twinkling like the stars above our heads, the other starting to close and turn purple. He put his arm around me and we skipped and swayed back to our trailer.

I turned to look for Elvie, but she was gone.

The curved point of the veiner pressed down like a long metal fingernail, creating a half-moon shaped scallop. Lifting and pressing created another one, and another and another. A fish-scale pattern emerged, getting harder to see as blood seeped through the deep slices.

He kept his tools sharp.

Next was the slant chisel. Into the flesh, straight down to the bone. Unlike sycamore, this canvas was not so strong. It moved under his fingers, it tensed, it struggled. He did not know where it would bend, when it would break.

But he could learn.

A carp leapt from the skin, caught in a crimson lake. His hook was embedded in the roof of its mouth, and he pulled and pulled, and carved and cut, until he landed his prize fish.

He set to work on the other straight away. He always carved in pairs.

In the years that followed, we attended many fairs; Stow, Seamer, Priddy, Brough. But I longed to return to Appleby. Ma said it was too big, too dangerous. The year we went, a child got crushed to death by a stampede of startled ponies. But in my fifteenth year, almost a man by then and a head taller than her, she could no longer forbid me to do anything. I'd started living outside in Pa's trailer all year round, cooking on the fire, sleeping under the canopy of stars. I didn't want to live brick anymore. All the while, I was learning how to bend ribs, whittle spindles, carve, paint and gild.

I don't know why I was so certain I would see her there again, and why it hadn't occurred to me that she would most likely be at the other fairs, as by their nature they attracted all the travelling folk. But in the same way that I knew how to mix the right varnish that would bend and not crack, I knew she would be at Appleby and that she had been there every year, looking for me, the same way I was looking for her now. Pa had pitched up on the same plot as before, but in the few short years since my first visit, the field was now crowded with painted waggons, some of higher quality than others. I spotted a few of Pa's builds and even some of my own fledgling paintwork.

I recognised her family *vardo* straight away. It was painted with cherries and summer blossom, with golden pears and apples adorning the doors.

She was a woman now, of that there was no mistake. But I recognised her all the same.

'Jack Collins,' she called to me. 'How's brick life?'

I pulled myself up to my full height, puffed my chest out and willed the few downy hairs on my lip to bristle with manly pride.

'I don't live brick no more.'

She narrowed her eyes and beckoned me closer.

I came over to where she sat, on the steps of her waggon. She curled her finger, calling me closer still. She leant towards me and took a deep breath through her nose, inhaling my scent.

'You might sleep under the stars, Jack Collins, but you'll always be a *gorja* boy.'

She touched my cheek and the corner of her lip lifted, ever so slightly. 'And that's no good to me,' she sighed.

Movement in the waggon behind her made us both look up. A face appeared in at the glass, scowling under a shawl.

'You'se be off with yer now,' Elvie shouted, shooing me away. Just before I turned to leave, crestfallen, she whispered 'Meet me at the river, down the bottom of the meadow. I'll be there at sundown.'

The door to the waggon swung open, and I caught a glimpse of treasures unknown. Dried herbs, shiny kettles, wild flowers, and right at the very back, a bed big enough for two.

It was the waiting he couldn't stand. Wood didn't make him wait. But flesh was delicate, unpredictable. It had to heal before he was sure the carvings were true and it was time to paint. And, unlike wood, there was only so far he could cut, only so deep he could pierce, only so many layers of skin and fat he could slice before he reached the bone. Bone was useful, to be ground down into a fine dust and used to stabilise his colours. But bone was not, in his eyes, beautiful.

Once the gouges had healed, once the scabrous skin had peeled and flaked, and raw scar tissue presented itself to him, only then could he paint.

He painted freehand, whatever the canvas. He had no time for stencils or tracing. Ox-hair gripped in a tiny quill. If he was painting ponies, a single hair would be used to line out every stroke in the horse's mane. If he was painting fruit, he would use big, juicy swooshes of colour.

Today, he was painting a pair of eyes. Blue eyes that would forever stare at him, accusing, blaming, pleading. Eyes that looked into his soul and found only shame.

I stood in the shadow of a tree whose branches hung low over the river and watched the sun go down. Somehow I knew I mustn't be seen, that our meeting was secret, shameful even. And it thrilled me. Every now and then I heard splashes of laughter, a fiddle playing, a dog barking. When night came at the fairs, it was time to dance, to drink, to love, to fight. Tribes gathering by firelight to sing and share stories and satiate their lusts, the way they have since before time itself. Humanity at its most glorious.

I waited. The sun had fully dipped behind the horizon, taking with it all the warmth of the day.

I waited. She wasn't coming. It was a trick. Silly *gorja* boy, falling in love with a traveller girl. He imagined her bragging to her cousins, telling them how she had left the fool down by the river, waiting for a sweetheart who would never come. I imagined they were watching me, through the hawthorn bushes, stifling laughter behind their hands. I turned away from the riverbank to head back up the hill towards camp, when I heard a thud of footsteps and a jingling of tiny golden bells.

'Where do you think you're going, Jack Collins?'

'Come to tease me some more, have you?' My voice was bitter as crab-apples.

'Tease you? I've been trying to get away. My brothers, they won't let me out of their sight.'

I wavered. Should I believe her? I pictured those same brothers, hiding just over the ridge, waiting to jump out and push me in the river, hold me under and drown me in horse piss and spilled beer.

'Well, ain't yer gonna talk to me now, Jack Collins? I thought we was friends, you and me?'

'Are you alone?'

'Course I am. You know what else I am? Cold.'

She moved towards me just as the clouds parted, letting moonlight spill over her face, illuminating her skin like a painted figure on a waggon. Her hair drawn in single strokes of charcoal, her lips stained with orchard fruit, her sapphire eyes. She pressed herself against me and I rested my fingers on her bare shoulders.

'My brothers...if they catch us, they'll kill me. Kill both of us.'

Our lips grazed.

'Do you ever wish you were someone else?'

'All the time,' I whispered into her hair. 'All the time.'

The pliers were heavy in his palm, carrying much more weight than any of his specialist painting and carving tools. There was nothing special about these brutes, they had one purpose and one purpose only.

Gold.

He yanked and twisted with all his strength, both hands around the grips, jamming his knee into the bed. A neighbouring tooth cracked and hot blood welled up over his fingers. With a final pull, the gold was extracted from the cavernous mouth-mine. He held the tooth up, marvelling at the length of the roots. Gelatinous blobs of spittle and gore plopped onto the bed. He turned the tooth upside down, so it now resembled a tiny, golden crown.

'Jack Collins, King of the Gypsies,' he laughed, but the words come out as a mangled mess.

Those days at Appleby were the greatest of my life. Rolling and riding under the cover of night, catching stolen smiles over campfires. Our secret love blossomed, as only the love between two young people can in less than a week. But my father and I still had business to do, and we were trusted by the travelling folk, as much as they ever trusted *gorjas*. I wanted Elvie to tell me everything about life on the road; the turnpikes and traditions, what they ate, how they slept, what they did when they were sick. I wanted to know The Way.

'I'd give anything to be that free,' I told her one night, my hand cupping her naked breast, our skin still slick and sticky.

'I'll never be free.'

'Come with me,' I said, the thought thundering through me on horses' hooves. 'Come with me tonight. We'll take my Pa's trailer and go, live together on the road. I can learn The Way…'

'You don't understand Jack, this way, this life, it's not for you.'

'I want it to be, please Elvie, I want it to be so much. Why are we so different?'

She sat up, gathering her clothes and brushing herself free of grass and leaves.

'I'm not a pony, Jack. You can't come to the fair and take yourself home a little piece of The Way and think it makes you one of us, it doesn't work like that.'

She wrapped her shawl around her shoulders and ran.

I wish that had been the last time I saw her.

He never did learn The Way. So he made his own Way. He kept his tools sharp. He looked for beauty in a dark world. Travelling, living the life of his dreams. But all he had were nightmares.

Then one day, his chisel slipped, carving a perfect line into the crease of his thumb joint. That feel of metal cutting through flesh, as soft and satisfying as catching an eel with his bare hands. He stared as the blood pumped itself out, flooding his palms.

And felt no pain.

He could smell wood smoke and summer blossoms on a night time breeze.

He remembered her, how she was.

Then, the pain came.

This was His Way.

It was the last night of the fair, and Pa was packing up so we could leave at dawn. I was gathering my tools, thinking about Elvie. I couldn't leave it like this, I might not see her again until the next Appleby. I swung my satchel over my shoulder and went to the meeting place, hoping she would be there one last time, despite our fight.

As I crested the hill, I heard screaming. No-one in the camp would have heard it over the noise of the fair, but down here her voice ring out over the river.

I started to run towards her, but then more voices joined in.

'*Gorja* with *gorja*, Rom with Rom,' they growled. I skidded low to the ground and hid behind the hawthorn.

There, next to the moonlight dappled water, was

Elvie, being held from behind by someone I couldn't see. The arm around her neck showed it to be a man, I guessed it must be one of her brothers. She struggled and kicked, trying to reach who I assumed was the other brother. He lifted a muscular arm and hefted his palm into her face. Her whole head whipped to the side.

'Little whore!'

I wanted to leap up, to run over there and save her. I had my bag, I kept my tools sharp. But instead, I lay there, a coward, hiding in the bushes. Elvie lifted her head, a thin line of red trickling from the corner of her mouth, the mouth that I had kissed not more than a few hours ago. Her eyes went over her brother's head, straight to where I was cowering. She couldn't know I was there.

But her eyes showed. She knew.

'Tomberon!' he shouted, spitting in her face. I knew this word. It was the worst thing you could call a woman, saying she was nothing more than a hole for men to fill. He drew his arm back and punched her again and again. When she was flopped so far forward that she had to be held around her waist to stop her falling to the floor, the fists stopped. He nodded to his brother, and Elvie dropped to the ground like a bunch of rags.

That was when the kicking started.

Gilding always came last.

He had worked on this creation for so many years, so much pain, so many scars. Yet it was never enough. He wanted beauty in a dark world. Beauty through his own suffering. It was what he deserved. Every slice was both punishment and blessed relied. Every chisel mark and veiner cut reminded him he was a spineless coward, weak and ashamed.

He had pulled out all his own teeth. At first for the gold fillings, then just because they were there and he didn't deserve them.

The eyes carved into his forehead were hers. Every day he painted them blue with leaded paint, hoping the headaches and sickness would not bring death by poisoning before he could finish. She stared out at him when he looked in the mirror, full of hateful silence and disappointment.

His tongue had been hard to cut out, but he no longer had a use for it. Life on the road demanded only the essentials. Any dead weight must be discarded.

He had made his own crucible from clay before he ripped each of his fingernails out with pliers. The crucible was now nestled deep in the fire, filled with gold teeth, his mother's wedding ring and one of the tiny golden bells he found on the ground when
Elvie's brothers had finally finished with her and rolled her into the river to wash up at a village downstream. Just a murdered gypsy girl with no name.

But he knew her name.

'Here's to you, Elvie Lee.'

He toasted her through raw gums and ragged tongue stump as he lifted the burning clay cup from the flames with iron tongs.

'Here's to you, my one true love.'

He opened his mouth wide as the liquid inferno poured over his face and into his throat, and he knew he had finally found The Way.

FIVE GOLD RINGS

1

Francine was my first wife. She was young and I was impatient. I harried that girl day and night to marry me. Every time I saw her at the corner store, buying groceries for her folks, I'd shout, 'When you gon' marry me, Miss Francine?'

She would just look down at the ground. But I could see her blushing, even through all them freckles. I turned up at the house one night, stood on that front porch with June bugs flying all around, and I called for her Pa. I asked for her hand in marriage, all proper like. He had eight mouths to feed, not including him and his cold-fish wife, so one less under his roof would be a blessing. He didn't even ask Francine, just told me I could have her.

We married in the spring, full of innocence. Francine at least. I knew what I was doin'. The first time I shoved myself inside her she was dry and scared, and she tried buck me off like a mad little mule. It never changed. I liked it that way. Her hair was so thin, it used to come away in my hands. I'll never forget the colour. Pale and clean as fresh bedsheets, and how it looked stained with blood like those same sheets on our wedding night.

I never meant for it to happen that way. The baby. The fall down the stairs that left us childless and her barren at eighteen. Such a clumsy girl, that one. Even her Pa used to say it. Always walking into somethin' or droppin' the goddamn groceries. When I saw her lying there, all bent and crooked, a bloody mess, screaming and crying, I got as hard as ever had in my whole rotten life. She was never the same after that. She didn't fight no more, just lay there, like a doll.

It was a sad day when she fell in front of that freight train.

2

Paulette was my second wife. I met her at the market, the handsome young widow. Everyone knew the story of my pale and crazy bride who took a leap in front of a train, stricken with grief. All the ladies in town got the soft eyes whenever I was around. There he goes, poor thing. I could look after him real good.

Boy, could that woman cook. I ate like a king when she was around. Coca-cola hams. Creamy mash potatoes and gravy. Peach cobbler. Buttermilk pancakes and candied bacon. I was fixin' to get fat as a stuck pig. My gut got so large I could barely see over it. She was a sturdy girl too. How her ass used to wobble when she ran away from me, how I could grab handfuls of overfilled sausage flesh when I finally caught up. I liked to bite into her, feel my teeth sliding through that buttery behind. She was meaty and creamy, like a fine steak.

I sure miss that Paulette. Shame she had such a smart mouth. Always running, like our old diesel genny. That genny needed a few good whacks with a wrench every now and again too, to keep it quiet.

Paulette don't run her mouth so much now it's fulla dirt and she's buried in the apple yard.

3

Lillie-May was my third wife. Met her at the roadhouse out on Breakneck Hill. She was a hellcat, that one. Thought she liked it rough. She had no idea. Daddy issues, that what they call it? Her Daddy was on his way to becoming a State Senator, had the money and the right connections. The only thing that stood in his way was that druggy dive-bar slut of a daughter. A career in politics means no skeletons in the closet. Or buried under the porch. Or wrapped in a blanket and rolled over a ravine.

Lillie-May loved to make her Daddy angry, to make him fret, and most of all, make him jealous. I saw the way his eyes lingered over her thighs when she wore them little shorts of hers. I could read his mind, picturing himself sliding a finger up inside them shorts, slipping it between her lips, then taking it out and getting a real good sniff of his daughter's delicious juices. And you know what? I think she saw it too. And I think she liked it.

We ran away to Reno. Eloping, she said. We sure are eloping, ain't we Big Daddy? She used to call me Big Daddy, and I used to call her Little Lillie Baby. See? That girl had issues. We partied, sniffed, snorted, drank and skanked our way through that marriage.

They found her dumped by the side of the road. I never broke her neck, but that pretty little skull of hers was sure smashed in after I'd finished with it.

I think I did her Daddy a favour.

4

Jackie was my fourth wife. Jackie, Jackie, O Jackie. Told her my name was Jack. Jack and Jackie, what a couple. Just like the Kennedys. I was new in town and she had a friendly face. She was one of them mousey types, you know the ones. Hair the colour they was born with, never wear a skirt over the knee, like helpin' the homeless and pretendin' they don't suck a dick. She said she had never met anyone like me before, I told her the same. I wasn't lying. I had never met a thirty year old woman who hadn't gotten drunk. I had never met a thirty year old woman who still had stuffed animals on her bed. I had never met a thirty year old woman who was savin' herself for the right man. I fixed all that in one goddamned night. Proposed to her over a cheap Mexican dinner and told her the cocktails were virgin, just like her. Took her tipsy ass home, dumped her on the bed and played stuff the animals 'til morning. She threw 'em all out soon after. Reckoned they smelled funny.

She used to talk about startin' a family, all her friends were expecting. Her friends thought I was cute. She did too, 'til I ripped her wedding dress. Fixin' to pack her things and go back to her mother that very night, she was. I took the lace veil from her hair, tied it round her neck and twisted 'til her eyes popped. O Jackie, you weren't expecting that.

5

Jack was my first husband. I knew that wasn't his name, just like mine wasn't Sally. Everyone has their secrets. We played house for a while, as the thunder clouds rolled. Oh, he had a cruel way and a dark eye, but he was handsome as The Devil. He said I was his one and only, and I believed him 'til the day I found four gold bands hidden in a beat up old tobaccy tin in his top drawer. One of the rings had a wisp of hair tied round it. The blood stain had long since turned from red to brown, but I knew it was blood all the same. I put those rings back where I found 'em and made believe like they weren't there. 'Til the first time he whipped me so hard with his belt that my back split in two. Then all I could think about was those four gold rings, and how I was as sure as goddamn not gonna be number five.

I was a good girl. I waited and watched. I listened and learned. Sure, I got a few bruises, but it was worth it. The time had to be right.

Jack was my only husband. I took a straight razor to his throat while he slept off a rotgut hangover, slicing through turkey-neck and vocal chords. And when he opened his eyes in shock, putting his hands up to stem the gushing blood, I took that razor downtown and cut off the only thing he ever really loved. His gurgles and spurts filled the air like wedding bells as I threaded five gold rings on his limp and bloodied dick, and threw it out the window.

'Til death do you part.

Ten Minute Warning

When it finally happened, after all the false alarms, all the scare tactics and practice drills and meals eaten from tins, breathing in each other's air for a few hours and thinking it a great adventure, when the siren finally sounded for real, we froze, paralysed as our pockets vibrated in simultaneous warning.

Would there be retaliation? Had the submarine commanders already confirmed the launch codes as we scurried into our well-stocked basement?

Would the warhead be shot out of the sky before it even reached us? Our allies were dwindling, and the ongoing war had left our defence budgets in tatters. Who would come to our rescue? Were we worth rescuing?

Would we feel the blast? We knew the missile was on its way, but where would it hit? A city? A village? A hospital? A school?

What would be the biggest killer? The fireball blast? The vaporising flash of light? The tonnes of dirt raining down from the mushroom cloud?

We were told to hide.

Hide and wait.

The fallout would be at its worst in the first two weeks, so the leaflets said. Plutonium particles carry for hundreds of miles on the nuclear winds, and I imagined them as sparkling dandelion seeds, dancing in the poisonous air outside. Our lungs would fill with the dust from a thousand cremated bones of our fellow country-men and women.

We had bottled water. We had board games and playing cards. We had blankets and pillows. We had first-aid kits with eye-baths and finger bandages and safety pins. We had each other.

So we waited.

The chemical toilet couldn't cope with all the corned beef and peaches we were eating, and blocked up around Day Five. The passing of the days was hard to gauge. My dad had covered up the tiny basement fanlight window with breeze blocks. We had battery-powered storm lamps for when the electricity went out. We yearned for daylight, for sunshine and clouds, and for cool night-time air.

Still we waited, our own stench filling our nostrils. We sponged our bodies down with disposable wet-wipes, which we piled into a plastic bag and left in the corner. The cot beds were uncomfortable, and every time I tried to sleep, I was woken by the ancient reflex that stopped our ancestors falling from the trees. My eyes opening with a jolt, I would see my father sat, staring at the pile of dried food packets. He seemed never to sleep, or he slept with his eyes open. I never could tell.

My brother was sick one day after a meal. We stopped calling them lunch, breakfast, dinner. Those labels were meaningless. Rice pudding, thick, white and lumpy, like curdled brains, came shooting out of his mouth and nose. My mother leapt to help him, cleaned him up, laid him down on his little bed. She thought I didn't see the looks passed over his head to my father, but I saw. I saw everything. We all did, down in that basement, together, all the time.

They said two weeks would be safe, and to listen to the radio for news.

We took a wind-up radio down there, but in all our drills and tests and play-acting the nuclear holocaust, we never stopped to check it actually worked. Faulty wiring, my dad said. In a way, I was glad. What would the radio say? Would it tell us how many died? How many lived? Or, even worse, would we crank the handle, build up enough charge, just for the radio to spew static back at us, mocking us with Geiger-counter cackles.

My mother brushed her hair and put on lipstick for the first few days, then the lips stayed bare, then the hair started to knot. When she tried to comb it, a limp, golden lock fell away in her hand. She hid it under her pillow, of all places. Perhaps she hoped the tooth fairy would take pity on her.

She didn't touch her hair after that.

My brother and I soon exhausted the supply of games, so we started to make up our own. Above ground, our age gap meant we were distant, strangers living in the same house. I found him annoying, he found me boring. At fifteen I was too old to want his spotty thirteen-year-old face around. But down here, in the prelude to the end of the world, or at least the world as we knew it, we became best friends again, like when we were small. We climbed around the room, pretending the floor was radioactive ooze, much to our parents' horror. We gave each other impossible "Would you rather..." challenges that made our mother blush and our father chuckle into his beard. I taught him silly dance routines and he shared his never-ending supply of knock-knock jokes.

When my father had counted fourteen periods of awake and asleep, he thought it safest to stay put, just for a while. We had no concept of day or night, hot or cold, apocalyptic doom or lucky escape.

So we waited.

We had enough food for months. All I wanted was an orange. I would lie in my cot, dreaming of peeling the fruit, piercing it with my thumb nail, the mist of citrus oil coating my skin. Of taking a bite, shredding the delicate flesh between my teeth. Of juice running down my chin and dripping onto the floor, despite my slurps and swallows.

I began to wonder what could grow from the nuclear ashes. Like volcanos produce fertile soil to nourish plants and trees, would this new scorched and dead earth eventually bring forth fruit? Would the pears droop on their branches, heavy with toxic sludge? Would the vineyards grow curly tendrils thick with bunches of blackened grapes that would burst like fish-eyes in your mouth? Would the carrots and potatoes buried underground claw their way out like zombies from their graves, white fingers of blight and mould facilitating their mobility?

I watched my brother. He watched me. He was hiding something under his blanket, I knew it. I saw my dad eyeing my brother's cot. He knew it too. What was under there? We subtly surveilled each other, never catching the other's eye, but aware all the same. He began talking to my mother in code. Although the surface conversations were about the water situation or if we should eat the tinned potato salad or the luncheon meat, it was obvious they were talking about me. They were planning something.

My brother was in on it too.

I had a revelation. He was hiding weapons; weapons we would surely need when we emerged into the wasteland of radiation survival. Guns and ammo? Maybe something more practical. A machete? An axe? Why had my parents entrusted my brother with our safety? He was too young. I was taller and braver. I should be the one to bear arms when we escaped our basement prison.

When the storm lamps were turned down low and my family's breathing had become shallow and deep, I crawled out of my cot, slithered across the floor and ran a hand under my brother's blanket. He grabbed my wrist. His eyes shone in the semi-darkness.

'I know you are in on it with them,' he hissed in my ear. 'I'm watching you.'

I melted back to my own lair, planning my next move. His eyes remained open, staring at me. Now I knew why they had given him the axe. It must be an axe, no-one would give a gun to a child; that would be ridiculous. They had given him the axe to protect himself from me. I could hear them now, tapping Morse code messages to each other on the walls and the floor. One tap for Kill Her Now.

Two taps for Wait.

Luckily I could understand them. I wouldn't be the one who waited to be slaughtered in my own bed.

My mother coughed.

That was the signal.

The tapping grew more intense.

A shaft of blue light opened up as I leapt from my bed to charge at my brother, raining down blows on his head with a can of condensed milk. His screams were drowned by the thundering of steps and the roar of shouting. Gloved hands pulled me away. Haz-mat suits and helmets filled the room.

We were saved.

My brother was bleeding from his nose and mouth.

He never woke up.

But at least the war was over.

THE RAPE OF IVY HOUSE

'Mr. Gonputh? Mr. Gonputh, are you there?'

Anita Sparrowhawk rapped her knuckles on the door, dusting her fingers with splinters of ancient paint.

'I'm from the council. You've been awarded a grant, Mr. Gonputh. It's part of our Clean Green Energy drive. We are modernising nominated houses in the local area. Bring you into the 21st Century, eh?'

This one's not even made it to the 20th century yet, she thought to herself as she stepped back and stared up. Thickets of ivy completely obscured the upstairs windows. Not that anyone would be able to see through them. The single paned sashes were thick with grime and framed in rotten wood. The house was built in 1875 as testified by the stone plaque above the door, which sat in the middle of the square brick frontage with two windows either side at the top and bottom. It was just like a child's drawing of a cottage, if that drawing had been crumpled up and left in the bottom of a bin for a hundred and forty years.

'I've got a few leaflets here explaining everything. I'll pop them through the letterbox. It's very exciting and it won't cost you a penny.'

Anita paused, certain she saw a twitch of yellowed net curtain.

That always gets 'em, tight old buggers. I bet he's got fifty grand in out of date bank notes stuffed under his mattress.

'I will be back on Monday with the workmen so we can get started. Yes, it's all very, very exciting.'

'I don't want no electrickery,' the old man shouted through the crack in the door.

'You can't fight progress, Mr. Gonputh, and this is all for your benefit.'

'And I told you, I don't want no electrickery, now sling yer 'ook.'

He slammed the door and a large branch of ivy dislodged, showering Anita with dusty spores.

'If you could just let us inside Mr. Gonputh,' she spluttered, brushing dead leaves out of her hair. 'Then we can assess what needs to be done.'

She turned to the two workmen, who were eyeing the house with trepidation.

'If he won't let us in, we'll just have to find another way.'

She hoisted her handbag defiantly over her shoulder and fought her way through the overgrown front garden.

Sat at his kitchen table he could hear her rustling and bustling, trying to find another door. *Good luck wi' that*, he thought. The back door hadn't been opened since The War. His memory got hazy when he tried to remember which one. The kettle on the coal range started to whistle. Stan Gonputh hoisted himself out of his chair and shuffled over, taking the threadbare linen from the front of the stove to protect his hand. As he was pouring water into his well-seasoned teapot (some would say dirty, he would disagree), Stan heard a muffled 'Shit!' from the rear of the cottage, and he chuckled to himself. *That'll be the coal bunker.*

Anita Sparrowhawk rubbed her bruised hip and leaned back in her fully adjustable lumbar-supporting ergonomic office chair. She had a migraine coming, and when she closed her eyes the black and white zig-zag patterns at the edge of her vision danced and jerked. Pinching the bridge of her nose, she shouted across the open plan office.

'Anyone got any ideas how to get a stubborn old git out of his house long enough so we can get in and do the necessary?'

'Has he got any family?' someone called back.

'No. He was married once. She died.'

'Perfect.'

Stan Gonputh turned up the wick of his handheld oil lamp and stared into the eyes of the only woman he ever loved. His Mary. His golden morning. His pretty petal. He didn't come up to see her as often as he used to. He found it hard to get around now his knees were shot. His joints screamed in pain, his legs were bandy and bent. But today he climbed those stairs. He needed to see her. To talk to her, like he used to.

'I'm keeping my promise, petal.'

She didn't answer. She never answered. Her mouth was a thin, grey slash.

'They're trying to get in, but I won't let 'em. It's just us here, eh petal? We don't need no-one else.'

Silence.

'And we don't need no electrickery, right?'

The flame inside the lamp flickered, causing a shadow to jump over Mary's cheeks. That was all Stan needed. She heard him. She knew he was keeping his promise.

The promise he had made before her light snuffed out forever.

The following week, Anita Sparrowhawk trotted up the path to Ivy House using a lever-arch folder like a machete, slashing away at the overgrown grass and weeds. The bruising from her collision with the coal shed had faded, but her indignant need to get this man out of his house had not. *Why won't these silly old fools just let me do what's best for them?*

'Mr. Gonputh? Mr. Gonputh, I really wish you would open the door. I just want to talk. No harm in a little chat, hmm?'

She was not taking no for an answer today and continued to bang her fist on the door. Her wide-brimmed summer hat had gathered some strange looks from the neighbours, but it now protected her from the shower of dead leaves and wasp carcasses that fell as she hammered on the wood. Eventually, the door shuddered open and a pair of eyes magnified behind thick glasses peered out.

'You again? I thought I told you…'

'And I told you Mr. Gonputh, this is for your own good.'

Two thick-necked thugs in white uniforms appeared from behind her and barged their way into the house, almost pushing Stan to the floor. A muscular arm scooped him up and two hands gripped his shoulders. He attempted to twist out of their hold, but the hands clamped down so hard he thought his collar bone might snap.

'Don't try to fight, Mr. Gonputh, you'll only make it worse. I have a court order here allowing me to enter your home and assess your health and wellbeing.'

She brandished a piece of paper in front of his face. It could have been her shopping list for all he knew.

'These two gentlemen are fully qualified carers, they will sit with you while I take a tour of the premises and complete a twenty-one point checklist of health and safety requirements before the workmen can move in.'

Anita took a cursory glance around the dim kitchen.

'Of course, you won't be able to live here while the renovations are being completed.'

'But this is my 'ouse! It's always been my 'ouse. I was born 'ere and I'll die 'ere.'

The bouncer in ill-fitting whites who held Stan in his chair glared down at him. The message was clear. *That can be arranged.*

'Now, now. Don't be silly Mr. Gonputh. Just think of it as a nice holiday. I've got a brochure here. You will be staying at The Pleasant Rest Care Home.'

'Peasant's Rest? That's where they send poor folk to die. You go in there, you never come out again.' Stan tried to stand and follow Anita, who was now squeezing her buttocks past a pile of newspapers and into the dark hallway. A hand the size of a bunch of bananas pushed him back down.

'You'll stay there, Gramps, if you know what's good for you.'

He doesn't know what's good for him, thought Anita as she felt her way through the gloom, *that's the problem.* Her fingers brushed against a door and she reached down for the handle. This would be the room known as the parlour, used by the Victorian residents of Ivy House for entertaining and high tea.

The stiffness of the door in the frame suggested it had not been visited for some time. She gave it a shove and a gust of stale air puffed out. The room was in black, with only a slit of light coming from edges of the thickly curtained window. Anita took four paces across the room and ripped the drapes open in a flurry of dust. She coughed, her eyes tight shut, tears streaming down her cheeks. When the wheezing and spluttering subsided she opened her eyes, expecting to see a room crammed full of worthless trash. Instead, she was staring into the eyes of a young child. She fell back, colliding with a dresser causing the china within to rattle. She clutched her hand to her chest, her heart thudding hard against her fist. A life-size portrait of a golden haired boy hung above a fireplace black with decades of soot. A teary-eyed cherub, his lips were thick and pouty as if he had just been scolded. Anita rubbed grit from her own watering eyes, and looked around the room. It was filled with portraits of the same sad, strange child. They were hung on faded William Morris wallpaper and propped up against walls. Small canvases were stacked on shelves and a series of cameos in silhouette were lined up on a mantel inch-thick with grey ash. Peering closer at the three oval frames, Anita saw only one was of the boy, the other two were a man and a woman. A mother and father. Parents and child. The eternal triangle.

A commotion in the hallway caused Anita to turn just as one side of the triangle came bursting through the door.

'You get out of 'ere! This ain't for youse, so get out!'

Stan snatched up an ancient chenille cloth from the table in the corner and tried to cover up the biggest of the portraits, but his efforts were cut off by a solid fist to his jaw.

'Don't do that you animal! You'll kill him,' Anita yelled as the old man's eyes rolled back in his head and he crumpled to the floor with a thud and a puff of dust. The last thing he saw was the blue-eyed boy that never was.

He always came to Stan in dreams, but the older he got the harder he found it to sleep. The punch had knocked him out cold, and for that he was grateful. She was there too, looking as beautiful as the day he met her, before she became a living ghost. It started with the painting. Mary was such a talented artist. She used to paint portraits of their friends. Just for fun, she never took any money. *Painting is my pastime,* she used to say, *not my profession.* Stan would ask her, *what you passing the time 'til, petal?* And she would always reply, *'til I become a mother.*

But the time passed. And still she painted.

Soon the friends stopped coming to visit. They had families of their own. Friends went off to war, friends died, friends came back with pieces missing. Some of those pieces were obvious in their absence, others not so much.

And still she painted. She painted Stan. She painted herself. But most of all she painted him. The perfect golden-haired angel who never cried, never spat out his milk, never broke his toys, never kicked his mother, never woke in the night.

The perfect child who never existed. Not at first anyway.

The two workmen, Darren and Terry, took up residency that very afternoon. Now Stan was out of the way, they could get to clearing the years of accumulated shit out of this dump and make it habitable for human life again. Thick insulation boards to cover the original walls, loft lagging, a telephone line and Wi-Fi, rip out the fire places and replace them with eco-friendly faux log burners, and of course fully wiring the house up to the mains. Electric lights, electric heating, electric oven, microwave, dishwasher and fridge-freezer.

'Lucky old bastard,' Terry said as they filled the newly delivered skip with junk. 'I wish someone would come to my house and give me a load of free stuff.'

The kitchen was easy. Everything had to go. Floors were ripped up, holes smashed in walls, ceilings yanked down. The rape of Ivy House had begun. When they got to the parlour, the face of the flax-haired boy shone down upon them. Without knowing if the paintings were worth anything or not, Darren moved them out of the room and piled them unceremoniously at the bottom of the stairs. Battery operated clip lamps were soon attached to the woodworm ridden bannisters and around the tops of doorframes. The corners of rooms were now shadowed in dark relief to the harsh artificial light. Spiders scuttled under skirting boards and mice cowered in tiny gaps in the walls. Darren shone a torch upstairs, but thought better of venturing up there. The risers were covered in threadbare carpet and the wood underneath probably rotten. Plus he had heard stories about this house. Stories that got passed around the village when he was a kid, embellished each time so that truth was lost long ago. All he knew was, he didn't want to be the first one to find out what was waiting at the top of those stairs.

Stan Gonputh lay with starchy sheets over his head, not moving, barely breathing. If he stayed motionless long enough, one of two things was bound to happen. Either she would bugger off and leave him in peace, or she would think he had finally karked it and set off some bloody alarm sending every nurse and his dog running into the room.

'It's no use pretending I'm not here Mr. Gonputh. The sooner you sign these papers, the sooner you can get back to your home. That'll be nice, won't it?'

Anita Sparrowhawk's voice was as sweet as a Diet Coke enema, and just as unpleasant. She was sick of his games. Sick of his stubbornness. Sick of the sheer bloody-minded pointlessness of his objections. She had decided weeks ago that he was just being obstructive for the sake of it. There could be no other explanation. The renovations to his house were not only free, but the solar panels would save him money on his future electricity bills and might even make him some money, allowing him to sell energy back to the National Grid. You'd think the tight-fisted old grunion would be grateful. But no, each time she argued with him, he came back with the same old line.

'I don't want no electrickery.'

So in the end, she lied.

'Mr. Gonputh.'

She laid a hand on top of the bedcovers where she imagined his shoulder to be.

'Stan. The council has listened to your concerns and have agreed that wiring the house up to mains electricity will no longer form part of the planned eco-upgrade. They're going to put in a wind-powered generator instead.'

She heard a soft rustle underneath the sheet. *I've got him.*

'Yes, they are going to install a small wind-turbine on your roof. You won't even be able to see it. But it will be enough to power the appliances that we are putting in. Appliances that will make your life easier, Stan. All of this will make life better for you, I promise.'

A tuft of white hair emerged at the top of the bed, followed by the thick black rim of Stan's glasses.

'But it won't be electrickery, right? We won't be hooked up to nothing? It'll just be the wind making my 'pliances work?'

'Of course. Now sign here, there's a love, and you'll be back home in no time.'

Stan thought back to the promise he made. The promise Mary begged him to make with her dying breath. *He told me Stan,* she had croaked in his ear. *He told me not to let them hook us up to the electric lights. He said Mother, you must'nt...*

He remembered cutting her off, even as sick as she was, angry that she was keeping up this stupid charade. *There 'aint no one to call you Mother. There is no boy. There never was.* The guilt he had at shouting her down, of yelling at his dying wife in her final hours never left him. But he had long since had enough of hearing about the boy. Had enough of looking at his face in those paintings. Had enough of feeling the child brush past him when he was in bed at night, sending prickles over his skin and freezing the very breath in his throat. *Promise me,* she hissed through gritted teeth speckled with blood. *Promise him. Promise your son that you won't ever get the electrickery.*

I promise, petal. I promise.

Work on Ivy House increased in pace. The council had an allocated fund per nominated house, but the quicker and cheaper they could get the job done, the more of the money they could funnel back into the council coffers. Although the workmen were on a day rate, they didn't realise their foreman had signed a contract meaning they would only get paid if the work was completed on time. For every day over the deadline, they would have money deducted. So the time had come for work to begin upstairs.

'You know what they say about this house?' Darren shouted up at Terry, who was clipping lamps at the top of the stairs.

'I know what *I* say about this house,' Terry yelled back down. 'I'm sick of the sight of it. Sooner we get done the better. I wanna get paid.'

'They say the old boy who lived here…'

'Lives here,' Terry interrupted. 'He ain't dead yet.'

He flicked a switch, flooding the landing with light. Darren peered up the stairs, his face pale.

'When I was a kid, they used to say he kept his dead wife up there.'

'Bullshit,' Terry laughed. 'Now get your arse up here and bring that loft lagging.'

Darren started to heave a large roll of insulation up the stairs with a grunt, pausing on each step.

'We used to hear him up there, talking to her. In the summer, when the windows were open.'

Step.

'It used to be a dare. Who could get closest to the house.'

Step.

'My mate Trev climbed up on that old coal shed round the back once.'

Step.

'I watched him pull himself up on the window sill. He was always a strong one, Trev. He pulled himself up just enough to see in.'

Step.

'He saw her, Terry. He saw the wife. I've never seen anyone so scared in my life. He screamed and dropped down on the coal bunker. Twisted his bloody ankle, but he didn't care. He just kept saying he saw her. The dead wife, Terry, she's here.'

Terry leaned down to take the lagging from his younger, and more gullible, workmate.

'He was having you on, Daz. There is no dead wife. Now stop being a pillock, I'll bring up the tool bags and you find the loft hatch.'

Alone on the landing, the light should have been a comfort to Darren, but instead it threw sinister shapes and created giant shadow cobwebs. He looked up, hoping he would see the small square door cut in the ceiling above him, but no. He would have to go into the bedrooms and check. He waited for Terry to come back up, but could hear he was now deep in conversation on the phone. Picking up one of the clip lamps, Darren peered into the nearest room. A pale death mask shone back at him. A woman long dead, her skin grey and peeling. He yelped and dropped the lamp on his foot.

'What are you squealing about, you big fanny?' Terry had arrived at the top of the stairs to see Darren cowering in the corner.

'Dead wife! In there…she's…in there.'

Darren pointed a shaking finger towards the bedroom where he had seen the ghost of Mary

Gonputh. Terry pushed the door open and shook his head in laughter. A half-finished portrait of a woman in dried-up oils stared accusingly out at them both.

'Turn her round will you Daz? I can't work with her looking at me.'

The day Stan Gonputh returned to Ivy House, nothing much looked different from the outside. He squinted up at the eaves and chimney to see any sign of the windmill, but that Sparrowhawk woman did say it would be discreet. Once inside, however, Stan didn't recognise the rooms he had lived in his whole life. Gone were the cool, gently worn flagstone floors, covered over with springy oak laminate. Gone were the blackened glass oil lamps, replaced with energy saving light bulbs. Gone was the coal fired range that his own mother used to heat his bath water when he was a small child, splashing in the tin tub in front of the fire. All his memories, all the physical landmarks of his life in Ivy House were gone. The walls had been painted magnolia in a slapdash manner that left splatters on the door frames and floors. He could see the dotted and dabbed plasterboard underneath where the walls had come down to make room for the cables. Cables that, Stan Gonputh had been assured, were not hooked up to the National Grid. He stared at the new microwave. It stared back expressionless, a blank faced robot. A futuristic intruder in his home. He wanted a brew, but the pristine white electric kettle looked too delicate for his gnarled old hands. Tired in the way only a nearly ninety-year old man could be, he wanted to be back in his own bed after the hard institutional slab he had been sleeping on at Pleasant Rest. He trudged through to the hallway, reaching for the oil lamp that wasn't there anymore.

He stood at the foot of the stairs and flicked the light switch. The bulb at the top instantly illuminated the shady corners of Ivy House with a ping. *Maybe this electric thing might not be so bad after all.*

Electrical current flowed through the newly fitted consumer unit and into the maze of cables that now circuited the house like a network of nerves. Anita Sparrowhawk had lied. A white lie. No harm could come of telling some old codger a fib. She slept happily in her bed, her conscience clear, as flames licked out from inside the metal box in Stan Gonputh's basement. The unit had been installed in a rush, and a single screw had not been correctly fastened, causing faulty connections inside the distributor box. The fire quickly spread to a pile of old papers that had been chucked into the basement during the renovation. Landmark news stories from as far back as the 1930s went up like dry tinder and burned a path all the way up the cellar stairs to the ground floor. The plastic underlay between the original floor and the laminate quickly melted and the newly painted doors began to bubble and warp in the heat.

'Father! Father! Wake up!'

The boy's voice came to him in his dream. He even felt the familiar tug at his arm in the moment between sleeping and waking.

You ain't real, Stan Gonputh said sternly inside his head. *You ain't real so leave me alone.*

Smoke soon tickled its way under his bedroom door. The fumes filled Stan's sleeping lungs, and he was dead before the flames ripped through the top floor leaving nothing but a blackened shell.

When the firemen combed through the burned wreckage of Ivy House, the only thing untouched by the fire was a portrait of a handsome young couple and their smiling, golden-haired son.

The Tiger & The Lamb

Information Wanted:

Female, 22 years, 5 ft. 6 in, 118 lbs, black hair, green eyes, very attractive, bad lower teeth, fingernails chewed to quick. Found naked, brutally murdered, body severed and mutilated. Subject last seen getting out of car at Biltmore Hotel. At that time she was wearing black suit, white fluffy blouse, black suede high-heeled shoes, nylon stockings, white gloves, and carried black plastic handbag, in which she had black address book. Subject readily makes friends with both sexes and frequented cocktail bars and night spots. Inquiry should be made at all hotels, motels, apartment houses, cocktail bars and lounges, night clubs to ascertain whereabouts of victim between dates mentioned. In conversations subject identified herself as Elizabeth or "Beth" Short.

LAPD Daily Bulletin January 21st 1947

He said I only had to change one thing, and that thing was everything.

So that's what I did.

On an LA day as hot as buttered toast, I wilted in line with all the other wannabes and usedtobes and nevergonnabes. Hollywood is no place for a girl like you, they told me. But I can assure you, Mr Zanuck, there is no other girl like me. I'm going to be a star. No, not a star, *the* star. I'm not just a pretty face.

Why, yes, thank you, mine *is* a pretty face. But I'm an actor.

No, I didn't mean actress. I meant actor. I take my acting classes very seriously. We have to be prepared to bleed for our craft, Mr Zanuck. That's what separates the shooting stars from the fallen fireworks. My teacher, like the best, finest surgeon, cuts us open and lays us bare. That is how we learn to cry, to love, to hate, all for the audience. He takes what is inside and presents it to the world, do you see?

They all come to me with their filthy problems, their monthly issues and inconvenient pregnancies. Their venereal disease. Diseases of Venus? Ha! These girls are anything but goddesses. They ask for prophylactics and spermicides and all sorts of other things that good, clean girls would never know about. They tell me stories of the casting couch and how they are always one screw away from the role that make them a star.

But the screw is always just that – a screw. Hard and cold and and twisted. If every girl in Hollywood got a starring role when she screwed a man who promised the world, there would be more movies being made than there are theatres to play them in.

I only promise one thing, and I always deliver.

This is going to hurt.

What's in a name? Shakespeare said a rose was still a rose, whatever you call it.

Yes, I know Shakespeare. Why are you laughing? I told you, I'm an actor. Anyway, Mr Shakespeare was right. I was a garden rosebud, all shy and shady pink. Now I'm a white rose in bloom. Fresh and new, all past sins forgiven, if not forgotten.

That girl is gone. Her story was mine, but now I leave her behind, shed my skin.

All you have to change is everything. Even my own mother wouldn't recognise me now. She didn't always know who I was before, and she often didn't care. But now she will know my name, they all will.

I'm ready for my close up. Come closer.

Closer still.

Do you see?

I'm a magician. I can pull a rabbit out of a black top hat. I can cut a woman in half. And nobody knows how.

I could stalk the humid Hollywood streets, ripe with putrid fruit, all painted red and bleached white as bone, like another magician, a kindred spirit of times gone by, in his hat and cloak.

But instead, they come to me.

The thick, black leather of my doctors' bag is cracked and worn, from years of hinges opening and closing, opening and closing.

Open wide. Wider still.

Stirrups flash in the neon lights of Sunset Strip as I take up my scalpel.

Rope burns skin in a bare bulb lit basement as I take up my saw.

Sometimes I find it hard to sleep. Sometimes I find it hard to wake. Sometimes I find it hard to live.

The doctor helps me. He always has the right pill, like magic. White ones, of course. Only the purest snow for the white rose.

The white rose must work. I can't grow, they won't let me. They keep me dead-headed, my roots twisted as vines, my petals fluttering in the fake breeze. There is no shade, only sun, that brightest of stars.

So here I am, in the hothouse, surrounded by the other flowers, but alone. Always alone.

Oh sure, he says he loves me, like the one before and the one before that. They adore me, they worship me. All eyes are on me, fifty feet high and lit from above.

Do you see me, I ask him. With those big, thick glasses of yours, do you really see?

She came to me once, they all did at one time or another. Those tramps with their cramps, their bleeding and their feeding. I shower them with diet pills and quiet pills and they totter away, back to their sweat stained hotel rooms and mildewed bathrooms.

She was just plain old mousy brown Norma-Jean. She didn't glow, she didn't shine. I like my girls all alabaster and ebony, like little Snow Whites. I didn't even give her a second thought, I'll be honest.

Not like my one. My beautiful Beth.

The world thought they knew her. But they didn't. Not like I knew her.

Her fingernails, bitten, bleeding and sore.

The runs in her stockings, the twisted seams.

Her chronic cough. Her Baaston accent that only came out when she was angry or upset.

I liked to watch her cry, just as much as I liked to see her smile.

They called her The Black Dahlia. But she was more than a flower to me.

The world thinks they know me. But they don't.

I'm not even sure if I know me anymore.

Jack says... oh, wait, sorry. I can't talk about him. I forget sometimes. I get... foggy.

I know people think I'm dumb, just some dizzy, dumb blonde. But I am a serious person, I have aspirations and dreams, bigger than what this town thinks I'm capable of.

He believes in me. He sees me for who I am. But it's our secret, so you mustn't tell.

You must never tell.

In the moment before I make the first incision, I imagine opening up the flesh, only for sawdust to come pouring out like confetti. Here comes the bride, cut from side to side.

But once the knife goes in, what comes out is always blood. Not the rotting, clotting kind that leaks from them, no matter how many rags and pads they stuff up there. No, the blood that flows and drips like wine, that leaves crimson tear drops on their freckled shoulders.

I work carefully, precisely and at my own pace. A peaceful monster, happy in his toils.

Maybe now they will take me seriously.

In the moment before I swallow the first pill, my hands shaking, I imagine filling myself up, stuffed to the seams with tiny white capsules, chalky and dry, insulating the emptiness. The water spills over my chest as I gulp it down, dripping down my thighs and onto the bedsheets.

I just want to sleep. Peaceful and serene, under glass. A crystal coffin awaits me as the fog descends; fluffy clouds waiting to carry me away. There is pain, but it is distant, an echo from another room, another life.

I am a white rose on a silk pillow. No more thorns. I just want to sleep.

Maybe now they will take me seriously

Marilyn Monroe, the troubled beauty who failed to find happiness as Hollywood's brightest star, was discovered dead in her Brentwood home of an apparent overdose of sleeping pills. The blond, 36-year-old actress was nude, lying face down on her bed and clutching a telephone receiver in her hand when a psychiatrist broke into her room at 3:30 a.m. It was learned that medical authorities believed Miss Monroe had been in a depressed mood recently. She was unkempt and in need of a manicure and pedicure, indicating listlessness and a lack of interest in maintaining her usually glamorous appearance, the authorities added.

By mid-morning Sunday the crowds of reporters, photographers and friends cleared away from the officially sealed home where the tormented actress had spent her last hours.

All that was left behind for the eye of the curious were two stuffed toys belonging to Miss Monroe's dog, a tiger and a lamb, lying in the rear yard.

L.A. Times August 6th 1962

HERRING GIRL

There were only two ways for a woman to survive without a husband in Port Maidens. One was opening your legs for money. The other meant stinking of fish guts and blood, a stink no amount of icy water and black soap could ever wash away

Tara chose guts.

She was woken every day at dawn by the cooper banging indecently on the wall of her tiny wooden hut, banging and banging until all of her crew shouted that they were awake. Only then would he move on to the next hut. She would sit shoulder to shoulder with her bed-fellows, their hair still damp with night-sweat, binding their fingers by candlelight. But no matter how much cotton she wound, no matter how tightly, no matter how much blubber she painted on, the salt water would seep through, deep into the cracks of her red raw fingers. Her hands never got a chance to harden and heal, they remained soft and porous, unlike her heart. The pads swollen, her fingerprints a ruined mockery of loops and whorls.

In darkness she and her fellow fish-wives, married only to their monotonous daily rituals, head to the dock. Some are widows, their husbands lost to that bitter mistress The Sea. Some came and went like birds, here for a season then gone. Some returned, no questions asked. Some were so young, still to learn about the world. They went about their work with songs and laughter. Port Maidens would soon teach them sorrow.

Herring girls never got to sample their wares, their fish were salted, cured, barrelled and sent off to Russia, the land of vodka and peasant revolt. There was no revolt here. No vodka either. Just the unrelenting tide and that wretched odour that penetrated your clothes, burrowed under your skin and sank into your very bones. Tara knew, if she ever managed to escape Port Maidens, the tell-tale tang of the sea would follow her wherever she went, dragging her back like a rusty anchor.

In the first light, the crews of girls take their place at the gutting stations and watch the boats landing their overnight catch. Baskets of slippery herring are sluiced into long wooden troughs before them, scales flashing in the low morning sun. The cooper rains salt crystals down from above, to give some grip to the slick, and still living, fish. Tara liked to imagine it was snowing precious jewels. Sometimes she would let it flow over her hands, mesmerised by its crisp twinkling. A clip around the back of the head from the cooper soon broke her reverie.

When work began, the space above the glinting, gasping treasures was soon a flurry of quick cuts, snips and slices, of deft hands making sharp, swift nicks and slits. Their knives were small, but what they lacked in size, they made up for in their efficient violence. Jam the knife into the gut, twist and pull. Out tumble tubes and glands, purple, pulsating, pouring into piles below. Fling the carcass of the fish on top of its dead brothers and sisters. Repeat. Repent.

Jam the knife, twist the blade, pull the handle, pour the guts, fling the fish.

Keep in time, keep in line.

While she works, breathing in the salty air of the bay, she looks out at the waves and pictures herself walking into the sea all the way up to her chin. She can almost feel the ebb and pull of the undertow, lapping onto her face, stinging her eyes, as she continues her path, calm and patient, until the water covers her head completely. When would the panic begin, she wonders. When would the natural instinct to live, to breathe, to exist, finally kick in? She fantasises about taking a deep breath, hearing her lungs popping and crackling with the pressure, feeling the cold spread through her, filling up her emptiness with the eternity of water.

Neither daydreaming nor fish-gutting are to be undertaken lightly.

Tara knows the knife has slipped before she feels it, her fingers numbed by the ice cold catch in her hands. Her binding blooms red as a small pool of blood forms in the crease between her thumb and her hand. It drips down her arm and into the wooden bucket between her knees, mingling with the spilled blood of a hundred herrings, indistinguishable and indivisible.

Then, the pain. Oh god, the pain.

An intake of breath so sharp, Tara almost cuts herself again. She presses her hand to her aproned chest and reaches her other hand into her pocket for more binding. The cotton is yellowed and already damp, but it is all she has for now. The tears streaming down her face are less salty than her skin, and they clear a refreshing path to her dry lips. Tara winds the rags as tight as they will go, tighter still, until her hand is stiff as a starched collar, and then back to work.

Keep in time, keep in line, never show the pain.

Never show the pain.

The night seems to last forever. Tara lies motionless, drenched in her own sweat, petrified she will wake the girls crushed up next to her in the dark. Her body swells and contracts with every feverish breath, the seconds between exhalation and inhalation stretching into minutes, with the elasticity of time that comes only with sickness. Her limbs are lead plumb weights, dragging her down through the bed, through the wooden floor of the hut, right into the damp, sandy soil below. She dreams she is lying in a coffin, jolting awake only find she is still there, nailed in and surrounded on all sides by dead wood. The slice in her hand, cleaned and freshly bound before she retired now throbs in time with her heart. Electric pulses prickle up and down her arm. Horses hooves thunder on the tin roof above her. Cantering and whinnying, the horses pour down the side of the hut, pounding the wooden walls. One by one her crew began to call out, 'Awake, I'm awake.'

A wake. I'm a wake.

Tara tries to shout, tries to tell the horses, 'I'm a wake, too! I'm here, I'm a wake! I am the very celebration of my own death.' But her mouth refuses to open, and the horses keep coming. Surely one of their iron shoes will punch through the thin wood, kicking her in the head. Tara thrusts the fingers of her uninjured hand into her mouth and prises it open.

'Wake,' she whimpers. 'Wake.'

The horses move on to the next hut. Time for work.

The tea and bread sit heavily in her stomach as Tara takes her place at the gutting gulley, knife in her good hand. The first slop of herring fall past her face, as the muscles inside her constrict. The smell hits her nose as her mouth fills with saliva and a taste she cannot place. She gulps it down and scoops up her first fish. It couldn't be anyone else's luck but hers, as a hook hidden in the gill snags her finger, embedding itself in the flesh at the side of her nail.

She had done a poor job with her binding this morning, having barely the strength to hold the cotton. Her eyes go in and out of focus as she unwraps the thin shroud, her hands shaking as she tries to pull the hook free. It wasn't buried deep, she could see the graceful curve of metal under her skin, but the barbed end made it impossible. The only way was to cut it out. Tara hovers her knife over the hook, burning from within, flames rising up her chest, her neck, her face.

The cooper notices something is wrong, and he shines his crescent moon face down on Tara. He is as far away as the actual man in the moon. His mouth moves, his long chin bouncing up and down as his smooth, scimitar teeth repeatedly chomp together. The sound is muffled, Tara can only hear the rushing of the sea in her ears as vomit floods her mouth. The cooper continues barking as she runs to the privy.

In the foul silence of the privy shed, surrounded by the half-digested remains of her breakfast, Tara takes her knife to the hook. As she slides the barbs free, it catches on her ragged fingernail and the whole thing lifts, exposing a silvery shimmer underneath. Tara screams through gritted teeth as she pushes the nail back in place, wrapping her finger as quick and tight as she can. The cooper will soon come knocking.

Back to work.

Keep in time, keep in line. Never show the pain, never know your name.

Unable to eat. Sipping brown tinged water, sweating it out faster than she can drink. Hot. Cold.

Hotter. Hotter still. Freezing, teeth chattering, spine scratching, legs burning, arms aching. All fingernails now peeled and discarded on the floor of the hut, transparent shells of some exotic nut. Red hair in slick twists and knots, lying limp and lifeless on her face. Tara lifts her head, and long strands of it fall away. She sheds her apron, her shawl, her dress, her underskirt and her shift. She continues to shed, shaking and shivering in her cot until she has finally wriggled free of her skin.

Glistening and glorious, her eyes clear, her head no longer pounding, she slips through the door, past the barrels, past the cooper and the gutting and the gutting and the gutting.

Pebbles shift and part under her feet, creating a path. Morning sunlight glints on her scales as gulls cry overhead. She quickens her pace, the crunch of shells beneath her webbed toes and the delicious taste of freedom on her tongue as salt water rushes to greet her.

No last glance, no final turn of the head or dip of the shoulder. No looking to the past, only the endless possibility of the oceans.

The herring girl swims far away.

HANNAH'S STORY

Rebecca Rolfe was sick. Sick of the sea. Sick of the damp. Sick of the crew and their leery eyes. Sick of the rotten food crawling with weevils. She had endured the three month Atlantic crossing with good grace, but now she was just plain sick. Every roll and list of the ship made her head spin and her stomach drop. Out on deck to get some air, a rare occurrence due to the foul storms and treacherous waves that plagued their journey, the ship's masts put her in mind of the towering trees she had left behind. Her heart thudded against her ribs with panic, certain that she would never see the Virginian sky again.

When they finally docked in Plymouth it was June 1616. Rebecca could no longer hide away in her cabin, pining for Chesapeake Bay. She had work to do. It was her husband's role to entice the middle classes to the colonies, but the bait he would use, his secret weapon as decreed by The Company, was Rebecca. Rebecca Rolfe was not simply a good Christian wife and mother, she was also a native Powhatan once known as Matoaka. She was the tamed savage that all of London's polite society would be desperate to see, to touch, to smell, and she would be introduced to them all by her childhood nickname: Pocahontas.

The sickness Rebecca suffered on the journey stayed with her even once she was reacquainted with dry land. Tomocomo, the Powahatan medicine man who travelled with her to London and for whom she had named her son Thomas, offered Rebecca sinister concoctions made with bitter mushrooms but she always refused. She had to be seen to act in all ways at all times a civilised, Christian lady of good standing, and such herbal remedies were the Devil's work. She awoke one night to find the shaman standing over her, chanting in a secret tongue and invoking the spirits of their homeland. Rebecca shooed him away, hoping he didn't wake John. Once he was gone, she prayed to the old gods that Tomocomo's spells had worked.

On all their visits Rebecca had to make sure her exotic looks and savage ways were never threatening to the ladies, while being sufficiently enticing to the men. The outwardly pious would praise God in all His glory for taming this once wild creature. They would theorise about the thousands of Virginian heathens whose souls were to be taken into the fold of The Lord, washed clean of their sins and educated in the ways of Christian society. Inwardly though, they would fantasise about the feel of her burnt-sugar thighs wrapped around their waists and the spicy smell of her sex. What forbidden knowledge did she possess? What wanton acts could she perform?

All she had ever wanted, since she was a girl, was to make peace. Peace between her siblings and half-siblings, all sired by the Chief, squabbling over who was his favourite and who would lead the tribe when he was gone. Peace between her mother and the other women of the tribe, who were jealous of the closeness that Matoaka and her mother shared with Chief Powhatan. It was the Chief who bestowed upon her the nickname of Pocahontas or 'little wild one'. By the time Matoaka was born, her father was already an old man, but his craggy face would light up whenever she attended his longhouse, and it hurt her to see how it would darken whenever the Captains came near to her village. Their white faces were shocking, but not as shocking as the way they spoke to Matoaka's father and the way they treated her people. They built their Jamestown, named for a king who was not Powhatan, in a land that was not theirs and prayed to a god who lived in a house, rather than to the gods of the earth, the sky and the animals.

And so when little Matoaka saw the Captains and their families starving, she felt pity, not glee like her brothers and sisters, and would sneak dried meats and preserved squash out to the Jamestown residents. She remembered a young man with sores around his mouth and eyes black as pawpaw seeds, who spat at Matoaka and chased her off his step with a long wooden shouting stick. Once at a safe distance, she had watched the man pick up the parcel of food, his head hanging as he went back inside.

And still, all she wanted was to make peace. When the fighting broke out between the Powhatan people and the Captains Matoaka went to see her father, begging him to stop, but he refused. Matoaka listened while the Chief and his warriors discussed their plans to attack Jamestown. All the men coming and going throughout the day ignored the little girl, being as she was both female and still a child. That night she ran to Jamestown to tell the Captains, who knowing her as the girl who brought them food when they were starving, trusted it not to be a trick.

Little Matoaka rode back into the village early that morning with a Captain holding her tight to him on his saddle. He smelled of stale sweat and tobacco and of a life lived under a roof. Her kin gathered round the horse, staring up at Matoaka and the whiteman, unsure if they should be afraid for her or themselves.

Matoaka shouted for her father.

Chief Powhatan emerged from his house, bending slightly before straightening to his full height. He puffed out his broad, naked chest. Despite his age, he radiated power. It was in no doubt that he could kill the Captain with his bare hands for daring to enter his village so brazenly at a time of war.

Neither wanted to make the first move.

The tribe drew a collective breath when Matoaka called to her father, saying he must make peace with Jamestown. The Captains were men of the land as he was, but they came from a different land and had not yet learned how to live in balance like the Powhatan. They needed our help, she told him, our teaching and our mercy, not our weapons and our war.

Had it been any of his other children perched atop that horse telling him to grant mercy to the pale monsters from the sea, he would have merely laughed and thrown his axe at the whiteman's head. It would have been a dead shot between the eyes, cleaving his skull in two, splattering the child with blood. But it was his little wild one, his Pocahontas, and he could not bring himself to risk the throw. Could it be that this child of ten years was wiser than The Great Powhatan Chief? She who saw the best in people, had a way of making them feel safe, of making peace.

He walked to the horse, reached up and took his daughter in his arms, ignoring the Captain, and carried her back to his longhouse. He whispered something in Pocahontas ear before placing her gently on the ground and going inside without a backward glance. The little girl ran to the Captain, barely reaching the flanks of his horse, and told him in stilted English that Jamestown had one chance to do right by the Powhatan and if they lied, it would be war like no other.

No mercy. No teaching. No food. Just death for all whitemen.

The Captain tipped his hat towards the longhouse, turned his horse and trotted away, a smirk threatening the edge of his mouth.

The whitemen broke their promises, of course, and the Powhatan went to war. In retaliation, the English kidnapped Pocahontas. Her words had not made peace, but instead revealed the Chief's one weakness. The war raged on, and the Chief vowed he would not make the same mistake again. He left his daughter to languish as a prisoner of Jamestown, refusing to give in to the demands of her captors. Abandoned by her tribe and still wanting peace, only now from the relentless attempts of the colonists to save her soul, she finally gave in and agreed to be baptised. Matoaka went into the water that day, but Rebecca came out, having washed away more than just her sins. She no longer saw the best in people, but had learned to see them for who they truly were.

They had been in England six months when the time came to attend with King James. It was January, and while it was not yet cold enough to freeze the Thames there was a sprinkling of snow on the ground when they set off for Whitehall at dusk. Her black waistcoat had to be worn unfastened over her gown, as the rich English diet had caused her waistline to expand despite her constant sickness. She had thought that perhaps the Lord had blessed her and John with another child but her monthly blood continued to come, so she did not mention it to her husband. Tomocomo travelled with her to the Palace dressed in his traditional clothing. He stubbornly refused the offer of a coat to wear over his breech-cloth and hide leggings, and his chest remained bare under his turkey feather cloak. Inside the palace, hundreds of candles made the rooms stifling. While Tomocomo stood proud in his feathers, chest puffed out and head held high, Rebecca was burning up under her layers of heavy clothes. Rivulets of sweat pooled at the bottom of her spine, and she could barely put one foot in front of the other while being shown to her seat for the evening performance. Had the chair not been there she would have simply lain down on the floor. Her hair was damp under her beaver skin hat and she longed to rest her face against the cool flagstones. From somewhere behind her, Rebecca picked up a whispered conversation. In her feverish state, it seemed the conversation was happening inside her head. Perhaps it was.

'They say she still retains her savage ways for the husband.'

'I hear he has two more of the wretches at his lodgings. Claims their souls belong to the Lord, but I know who their filthy heathen bodies belong to.'

'And where is he tonight? Leaving his wife to attend the Palace of Whitehall with her naked medicine man, while he plays bishops and sinners with the nursemaids.'

'Indeed. And you would think she could have dressed her pet for meeting the King.'

No matter what she did, Rebecca would never be accepted here. She would be a curiosity at best, an enemy at worst. Tomocomo sat proud next to her, straight as a pine and oblivious to the sniping. He knew exactly who he was, so being different held no fear for him. Not Rebecca, or was she Matoaka? Or Pocahontas? Her brain was slow and gluey. Panic rose in her chest, the same panic from the crossing all those months ago. Her heart racing, her head spinning, like she was about to fall off the surface of the earth. Gripping the bottom of her chair to stop herself, eyes shut tight, she braced for impact.

Instead, a man's gentle voice in her ear, with no hint of the malice she had just overheard.

'My dear lady, I hope you enjoy the performance. Some advice, perhaps? Open your eyes, lest you miss it.'

She lifted her head to see the speaker and caught a glimpse of a soft-faced gentleman with a gingery beard and a bulbous nose seated next to her. At that moment all the candles were snuffed out simultaneously – no mean feat due to their sheer number – and the show began. At first she felt the eyes of her neighbour fixed on her, but she soon lost herself in the music.

After the performance Rebecca did a tour of the room, wondering which of the smiling faces had been damning her behind her back only a few short hours ago. She searched for her kindly fellow to tell him she had very much enjoyed the dancing and his advice had been sage indeed, but he was nowhere in sight. Tomocomo complained to Rebecca that they had yet to meet the King, a snub which he considered a personal insult.

'Chief Powhatan would never treat an honoured guest in such a way,' he complained in Algonquin.

'He would treat a guest better than his own blood,' Rebecca replied, surprising herself by speaking in her mother tongue.

Tomocomo nodded, taking this as high praise for the Chief. Rebecca was simply speaking from her own bitterly disappointing experience. A wave of nausea flooded over her. She pinched the back of her hand, hoping the pain would jolt her out of the sickness.

When the carriages came to take them back to their lodgings, Rebecca could not have been more relieved. The world was moving a heartbeat too fast, and she did not care that she had been denied the opportunity work her charms on King James. The opinion of The Company would be quite different. As Rebecca was about to climb into the carriage, she turned to their Palace escorts.

'Please thank the King for the wonderful sights and sounds we experienced here tonight. It is a grave shame that I did not get to attend with him in person.'

The escorts rolled their eyes. Had she been back in Virginia, their thoughts would have been clear as an icy stream, but now so far from home her ability to see the truth in people was clouded.

'But Mrs. Rolfe, His Majesty was seated beside you for the entire performance.'

The bone-deep winter finally passed, and by March The Company decided the Rolfes had done sufficient to secure their passage home. On the morning they were due to sail out of London, Rebecca was seized with a great pain which caused her to gasp and stumble while carrying young Thomas aboard the ship. The nursemaids immediately fussed over the child, taking him below decks. John stooped to help his wife up. There was no colour in her cheeks and a sheen of sweat covered her brow.

'My dearest Rebecca, what is wrong? Shall we call the physician?'

Rebecca gritted her teeth against the pain, assured John she was fine and that they were going to miss the tides if they did not hurry. All her dreams of late had been of Virginia, and she wanted nothing to stand in the way of her return. Once they were in open water, she would call for the ship's doctor.

They had barely passed Greenwich when Rebecca was gripped with agonizing pains again and sudden gush of blood between her legs. Despite all her protestations, John ordered the ship dock at the first available port. By the time they were tethered at Gravesend, Rebecca was haemorrhaging at an alarming rate and the nursemaid named Hannah was running out of blankets to soak up the blood. She ran back and forth taking away the blood soaked sheets, creating a dripping, gelatinous pile in the galley. Arm deep in blood, she suddenly pulled a tiny body out of Rebecca. Silence hit the cabin as they waited for a cry from the small mouth. It did not come. Hannah used a hooked knife to cut the cord with a fleshy crunch and took the pale, silent baby away. The physician finally stepped into the fray, took one look at the blood-sodden bed with its steadily congealing pools underneath.

'This woman needs a priest, not a doctor,' he said, before turning on his heel and walking out.

And there she died, nearly four thousand miles from home, aged just twenty-one. Her bones were laid to rest the very next day in the chalky earth of Gravesend. In her final hours she was no longer Rebecca, wife of John, mother of Thomas. She was not even Matoaka. She was something deeper, wilder. Pocahontas. The little girl who wanted to make peace.

Her final words, 'All must die, but 'tis enough that my child liveth'.

Whether Hannah heard these words or not, she did hear the faint gurgle and mewl from the bloody babe in her arms as she took it away. She looked down at the tiny purple face, and in the space of less than a second, saw her life panning out ahead of her. Now her Powhatan mistress was surely dead, how would she be treated by the Captain? John Rolfe was still a Captain in her eyes, a whiteman, nothing more.

After giving the baby a swift slap on the back to bring up any fluid, Hannah hid it under the pile of gory rags. In the kitchen she found a large onion and some hard-biscuit and wrapped them in a bloody cloth, all the while chanting under her breath. Hannah hurried back to the cabin, handing the dripping bundle to Sarah saying their mother tongue,

'It's the baby, so they can be laid in the ground together. I have to go ashore now, I can't bear to be on this ship of death any longer.'

She rushed back to the office of Captain Rolfe, where she found a small leather purse filled with coins. Grabbing the purse she ran down to the galley, picked up her precious cargo, and bolted for land. Hannah ran and ran, the realisation of what she had done creeping in. She would have to find some way of feeding the child – if she let it suckle her breast for long enough would milk come? She did not know. She had not nursed Thomas for weeks. He preferred Sarah now he was old enough to choose.

Her own baby, a girl she had named Nadie, meaning wise one, had died shortly after birth. Her husband had been killed fighting the Captains. She was all alone, which was how she had come to be nursemaid to young Thomas Rolfe. Hurit, her newly engorged breasts burning, had been immersed in cold water and given a new name, a place to live and a baby boy to nurse away both the fire in her breast and the sorrow in her heart.

Hannah, her chest burning now through lack of oxygen, stopped running and found herself outside an inn called The Flying Horse. With her head down, babe clutched tight to her breast, not even knowing yet if the child still lived, she entered.

'I…I need room?' she said, out of breath but in her best English, to whoever might be able to help her.

The landlord took one look at the curiously dark-skinned girl, who appeared to be covered in blood.

'You want The Mermaid'.

A tear popped over the bottom of Hannah's eyelid. She shook her head in confusion.

'The Mermaid,' he said again more forcefully, and pointed out of the door. 'You can't miss it, and there's plenty o'your type there.'

The patrons of the inn gave Hannah ugly eyes as she backed out of the door. She remembered childhood tales Ne Hwas, two sisters who had become trapped in the waters of a lake, who grew tails like sea-snakes and whose eyes turned to black obsidian. The tightly packed buildings bore down on her, enclosing her on all sides.

And there, painted on the weatherboard of a building on the other side of the dirt road, was a lusty looking wench with the tail of a fish, combing her hair without a care in the world. Hannah stumbled towards The Mermaid Tavern, hoping to find a home in this strange, new world.

LITTLE MISS COLORADO DREAM QUEEN

When the plane crashed into the only bridge out of town, Frankie Mackenzie was passed out in a puddle of her own dirty underwear. Her phone vibrated every couple of seconds, inching its way along the length of the dusty bedside table before plopping onto the floor next to her head. It was only the following day, when the kitchen tap stopped dripping onto the stack of plates in the sink that Frankie opened one eye. Her brain fired into life with a headache like a steel toe-cap to the temple. Before opening the other eye, she ran through her post-binge checklist.

Am I dressed? Yes.

Am I in jail? No.

Am I at home? Yes.

Am I alone? This was a tricky one. Who knew what horrors might be lurking in her bed. Frankie peered over the top of the stained mattress.

Empty.

Her phone continued to buzz by her knee. Snatching it up, the display showed sixty-two missed calls. She was about to answer when the phone went dead. Full battery. No signal. Frankie scrolled through her text messages.

Where are you?
Get here now!!!

Are you OK?
You'd better get to work NOW if you are still alive.

Whatever shit her boss was trying to pull, Frankie wasn't going to fall for it. She stuck her phone in the back pocket of her jeans and padded through to the kitchen. With every step she became more hunched over, as if her head yearned to be back on the floor. Lifting the receiver of the touch-tone phone, she was relieved to find the landline was dead too. That meant she had some time to straighten up before she had to speak to her editor, Everett Roscoe. Whatever story he wanted her to cover, it was sure to be the result of some poor soul's misfortune. Frankie was the worst kind of hack journalist. No story off limits, no ambulance she wouldn't chase, no grieving family member out of bounds. That was why Roscoe hired her. And why he ignored her frequent three-day 'Russian holidays'. Why he never mentioned that she smelled of Smirnoff rather than Chanel. Why he never commented if she was wearing mismatched shoes. In turn, Frankie put up with Roscoe rubbing up a little too closely when he passed her in the office, leering down her top at the coffee machine and the sticking in an unwanted tongue each New Year's Eve when they kissed at midnight. He had goosed, groped, fingered and frottaged every woman that came to work for him, and branded them frigid when they objected. Frankie had cut his advances dead so many times, he called her Mack The Knife. She called him

Roscoe The Sweaty Fat Fuck. Theirs was a relationship based on mutual understanding.

Whatever Roscoe wanted, she had better go and find out.

After a quick pit-sniff and a check for vomit stains down her top, she chucked on her ankle-length puffa jacket. Expecting to step out into the refreshing Colorado evening chill, she slammed the door and turned to find the world on fire.

Black smoke billowed from the direction of the bridge. Snowflakes mingled with ash in the air, creating grey drifts against the kerb. Sirens wailed in the distance. Doors of nearby houses hung open and cars stood abandoned in the street, their insipid warning sounds dinging away to no-one. A figure appeared in one of the doorways and began to shuffle over. It was an old woman with two rollers in the front of her hair, dressed in a flowery housecoat of the kind Frankie's grandmother used to wear.

'You're not going over to help look for survivors?' The woman was close enough now for Frankie to see she was barefoot. One of her eyes was swollen and sagging slightly, causing her cheek to bulge.

'Survivors from what?' Frankie asked. 'What happened?'

'They won't find anything but corpses, you mark my words. Even Saint Lawrence himself would have perished.'

The woman decorated herself with the shape of

the cross. Something seemed odd to Frankie, but her hungover brain was struggling to process what the woman was saying.

'Turn me over, I'm not done,' she continued. Her good eye stared through Frankie as if she wasn't there.

'I don't understand.'

'Saint Lawrence. Roasting in the fiery furnace on a spit of righteousness. That's what he said to the torturing sinners. Turn me over, I'm not done.'

The woman smiled up to the heavens, ash drifting onto her face and settling on her eyelashes.

'O-kaay,' said Frankie, backing away. 'I must have missed that one at Sunday School. And you still haven't told me what survivors you're talking about?'

The woman's face dropped, and it hit Frankie why the way she crossed herself was so strange. She had done it upside down. The woman tutted and a shadow moved under her nose.

'From the plane crash, you silly girl.'

An earwig crawled from her nostril and onto her top lip. Seized by the urge to flee, Frankie stumbled backwards over her own feet.

'Dont'cha wanna know what happened? Nosy little girl like you, always in other people's business? I'll tell you all about it, come inside.'

The woman sniffed, causing the earwig to shoot back up her nose. Frankie trotted away, mumbling about needing to be somewhere. Once she had rounded the corner and the creepy old bitch was out of sight, Frankie slowed down. Whatever had happened, Roscoe would tell her all about it and before giving her the most offensive angle for the subsequent story. Photos of dead children. Digging up dirt on the victim's private lives. Whatever scummy, lowlife, bottom-feeding piece of gutter-rag trash he wanted, she would write it.

Frankie had come to Colorado in the early Nineties, like many aspiring journalists, to investigate the infamous child murder in Boulder. Convinced she would be the one to break the case, she became frustrated at her lack of ability to find any new leads. So she slept with a couple of police officers to get some information. No big deal, she told herself. They were hot, and more than happy to spill details about the case over a post-fuck cigarette. She bugged the car of a family friend and even stole autopsy photos. Whatever it took to get justice for that poor little girl, found hog-tied and garrotted in her own basement. It was only when she started cornering kids outside the school that the Boulder Police Department got involved and she was slapped with a restraining order that meant jail if she came within one hundred yards of anything or anyone to do with the Ramsey family.

She picked the town of Hell purely by virtue of its ridiculous name and applied for a job at The Hell Star, submitting a portfolio of her freelance work, all written under the name Frank E. Mackenzie. It still brought a smile to her lips when she remembered

Roscoe's face as she walked into his office for the interview. A woman! A woman had written those stories with such cold detachment, even when reporting in grim detail the murder of an innocent child. He hired her on the spot, and she had been in Hell ever since. This little town had everything she needed, namely a newspaper, a liquor store and a couple of gas stations where she could pick up a pack of smokes.

The sign for Sandie's Gas came into view as the explosion knocked Frankie off her feet and into a snowdrift. A secondary blast wave sent a column of fire into the sky. The smell of gasoline mixed with the stench of cooking flesh and melting plastic. She ripped off her coat, screaming as it pulled away the skin on her back. The intense heat from the burning gas station made it hard for Frankie to open her eyes, but she rolled back into the snow with a hiss and assessed the scene of devastation in front of her. The flat roof of the gas station had been forced out at an acute angle and the glass from the windows was now strewn across the asphalt. It glittered in the flames, which were not only shooting up into the sky but also careering along the ground in waves. The sign for Sandie's Gas had been ripped off its post and was buried deep in the windscreen of a nearby car, now reading simply 'die'.

A mushroom cloud billowed upwards, raining down comets of fire. Lit from the flames below, the huge grey cloud looked flat and cartoonish. As

Frankie stared, the plumes of smoke and ash began swirling with black creatures, a tangle of flailing limbs and pointed wings. She grabbed two handfuls of snow, closed her eyes and rubbed them with ice. Opening them again, this was no hallucination.

Black bodies were swarming out of a chasm that had opened up on the scorched asphalt. Several of the creatures had broken free from the smoke column and were diving and wheeling in the sky. They had female forms with wings of taught black leather and slick, naked torsos. Their legs were covered with dark hair and one of them spun in mid-air revealing a long pinky-black tail with a vicious barb at the end. Frankie lay paralysed in the snow, hoping they didn't see her. More of the hideous harpies were pouring from the ground, chattering and screeching to each other over the roar of the burning gas pumps. Though their bodies were that of women, their faces showed them to be a mismatched troupe of chimeras. Some had hooked beaks for ripping flesh. Some had feathers, some had fur. Some had long ears protruding from the tops of their heads like raggedy hares. Some had faces like pigs with filth encrusted snouts.

Bracing for an attack, Frankie was relieved when the monstrous pig-bat women soared up to join their friends in the clouds, and the whole flock moved away with hive-mind synchronisation. Frankie came to her senses and managed to slip her phone out of her back pocket in time to snap some fuzzy pictures of the creatures before they disappeared into the night. Screw Roscoe and whatever reprehensible story he wanted. This was the story. Pig-rat harpies in the skies over Hell. Leaving her melted coat behind, Frankie packed some snow onto her blistered back and made a run for the newspaper office.

The Hell Star had been Frankie's second home for the last twenty years. She had seen reporters and office clerks come and go. She had made some friends, fucked a few of those friends, fucked over a few more of those friends, and watched everyone leave the rag for greener, and better paid, pastures. Only she and Roscoe always remained, the perpetual odd couple.

Frankie passed a few people on the way to The Hell Star, all with the same vacant look as Old Lady Earwig. By the time she arrived she was out of breath, viciously hung over and her back was a charred mess of pain. The office appeared dark from outside.

Frankie's scalp tightened. She got the keys out of her pocket, but as she went to put them in the lock, the door swung open. Someone was here.

In the dark.

'Roscoe?'

Frankie flicked the lights to the main open-plan office. The ancient fluorescent tube lights pinged a few times but refused to fire up. She was always telling Roscoe to replace them and now they had finally given up. A dim light was coming from the cramped landfill at the back that Roscoe called his office.

'Roscoe? I know you're here. Forget the plane crash, I've got the story of the century right here on my phone. You won't believe it!'

She swiped a cigarette from a half-smoked pack on her desk, lighting it with a shaking hand as she opened her top draw. A selection of miniatures lay there, twinkling up at her like precious jewels. Her pounding heart was calmed as soon as her fingers brushed the diamond glass of a tiny Absolut bottle. She drained it in one, and selected couple of Bombay Sapphires for luck.

'Listen Roscoe you mouth-breathing slob, I've got...'

Frankie's voice trailed off as she took in the scene before her, lit in silhouette from Roscoe's computer monitor. Her editor was reclined in his leather swivel chair, eyes closed, his face a picture of bliss. The top of a woman's head bobbed up and down in his crotch. Wet sucks and snuffles punctuated Roscoe's groans of pleasure. Only he could use a national tragedy as an excuse to get a blow job.

'Whoever that is down there, you can get off your knees now, honey,' Frankie shouted at the shape between Roscoe's legs. 'No promotion for you to swallow tonight.'

Roscoe spun his chair to face Frankie and the figure hunched over his thighs let out an ear-splitting screech. A pair of wings flapped under the desk. He stood, revealing a black cavern where his fat gut used to be. His intestines spooled out with a slick plop, and the smell of shit exploded as they hit the floor. Bile rose in Frankie's throat as the demon woman pounced on the innards, munching and slurping. Roscoe reached into the bloody ruin between his legs, plucked out a gristly lump of flesh and held it out to Frankie.

'This is what you want, isn't it Mack?' He jiggled the ragged collection of tubes and skin. 'It's what you've always wanted.'

Roscoe licked his lips with a black tongue and threw the mangled appendage at Frankie. She dodged out of the way as it skittered across the office carpet. The leathery creature under the desk stuck its ratty snout in the air, nostrils quivering and whiskers trembling. It flicked round to glare at Frankie, saggy mammaries swinging limply on its chest. Mangy feathers decorated its shoulders and neck. Greasy hair hung over its face, its elongated snout-mouth tipped with two yellow teeth. They made eye contact and the thing hissed.

'That's it girls,' Roscoe said, with his hand pumping furiously in the hole where his dick used to be. 'You two make friends. We can all have fun together.'

The rat-harpy spread her wings and clambered

onto the desk, claws scratching wood. Its tail whipped round, slicing Frankie across the face and waking her from her stupor. She felt the cool glass of the miniature bottles she was still holding, and in one smooth motion smashed them both onto the floor. Frankie dropped the lit cigarette from her lips as the creature jumped down from the desk.

'Suck my dick, Roscoe.'

A whoosh of flames filled the doorway as Frankie ran from the office. Lying between her and the exit was Roscoe's discarded penis, now oozing green slime and inching its way along the carpet like a caterpillar. She booted it out of the way with an expertly aimed toe-punt and bounded out of the door. More of the pig-bird women were gathering in the sky above. Spotting the paper-boy's BMX propped up outside, Frankie jumped on the bike and pedalled home, flicking up grey slush from the wheels. Her legs and lungs were burning when she abandoned the bike on the street outside her apartment building with a clatter, struggling to get her keys out and dropping them in the snow. Scrabbling around in front of her door, she heard the approaching swarm of flying rat bitches chittering and howling. Finally slotting in the key and twisting, she fell into the dark hall and slammed the door. She waited for the scratch of claws on wood. But it never came. Whatever those things were, they weren't after her. Frankie decided to pack a bag before they came back. It was time to get the fuck out of Hell.

Throwing a couple of t-shirts and a clean pair of underwear into a rucksack, Frankie headed for the liquor cupboard to get the only thing she really needed. Something about the dark kitchen was different yet strangely familiar. The tap was dripping again. The same green slime she had last seen seeping from Roscoe's mangled dick was now plopping in fat lumps into her sink. From the blackest corner of the kitchen, she heard a scratching sound. The rustling of polyester and lacy ruffles caked in grime. The shadow of long eyelashes brushing rosy cheeks. The smell of candy-apples in formaldehyde.

'Why did they kill me, Frankie?'

It was JonBenet Ramsey.

'Why won't anybody play with me?'

The tiny girl lifted a hand. Pink nail varnish glittered on the tips of her rotten fingers. Bare bone protruded from her knuckles as she curled her hand into a fist, held it under her chin and gave three little nods, a gesture that would have been cute when she was still alive. Miniature cowboy boots clicked on the linoleum, sequins flashing as she did a twirl, coming to a stop in front of Frankie. Her round, cherubic face was cratered and peeling. The perfect rosebud that was once her mouth, now blackened and dry, opened to reveal a mouthful of maggots instead of tiny tic-tac teeth. Frankie dropped the rucksack she was carrying with a smash and slumped to the floor. Now face to face, JonBenet gave a theatrical wink and held her hand out to Frankie.

'Will you be my friend?'

From somewhere outside Frankie heard a dull thump, followed by another and another and another. A ratty face slammed into the window. Scabrous wings flapped and scrabbled as more of the vile creatures piled themselves against the glass, now cracking under the strain.

Frankie looked into the blue eyes of the murdered girl, forever a broken china doll. She would never grow up, never get her period or kiss a boy and have her heart broken. She would never drink stolen whisky under the bleachers or stay out dancing 'til the sun came up.

'Sure JonBenet, I'll be your friend.'

She took the tiny hand in her own as the window splintered inwards and the first filthy succubus forced its way in.

ELVERS

1. BIRTH

One of Juno's earliest memories is sticking her hand into a bucket full of maggots. She couldn't have been more than three or four. She plunged her pudgy little arm in right up to the elbow, their dry wriggles and shudders caressing her skin. She remembers squealing with delight when her father would take one and place it between his lips. She used to watch, transfixed by every twist and squirm in their fruitless attempts to escape, as if they knew their fate was to be impaled on a hook and cast out, away from their thousands of writhing, roiling siblings.

She almost felt like she could remember her own birth, she had heard the tale so many times. How on a freezing February night, the night of the Snow Moon, her mother had been seized with pain. How her father had called for an ambulance, but none came, so he wrestled his howling wife into the car and sped to the hospital, not passing another vehicle or living soul on the way.

'It was as if a path had been cleared for us,' he would say when telling and retelling the story. 'As if the only thing that mattered in the whole world was getting to that hospital. We knew we were on the way to meet you, our precious moon baby. It was your mother's proudest, most joyful moment, despite the pain.'

That pride lasted a whole eight minutes, before her mother's uterus ruptured and an oxygen-starved Juno had to be ripped out of her mother's abdominal cavity. She eventually bled to death, leaving Juno's father a widower at twenty-five with a tiny, screaming, gore-streaked monster to look after. The on-call consultant had told him there would be a high chance of brain-damage before he ran off to get in an early morning round of golf. The line about the golf was always the punchline to the story, the bitter aftertaste of an experience too much for her father to bear without making a joke.

Juno swore she would never have kids.

Not that she would ever get the chance.

She hadn't always been afraid of men, but eighteen years of living with her father ruined any chance she ever had of forming a relationship with one. Her childhood had been idyllic, playing by the river, learning to fish, scooping up tadpoles in glass jars. But as soon as Juno started to show signs of tender teen-age; locking the bathroom door, hiding her budding breasts under thick jumpers, the shimmery pink lip-gloss and flowery body-spray, her father changed. They no longer had fun, no more rough and tumble, no more cuddles. It was as if her womanhood was contagious. He showed his love in other ways; plumping up her pillows before she went to bed, making her favourite dinners, checking if she was too hot or too cold, bringing her cups of tea. And always the constant warnings about BOYS.

Not boys. But BOYS. To be feared. To be avoided.

'You're special,' he would say. 'Too special for greedy, grabbing BOYS.'

What made her so special, her father would never tell.

'You'll find out one day, when you're grown.'

Being told she was special every day had not made her conceited as it might some girls. It made her scared, terrified even. But now she was grown, a woman of twenty-eight, and she was still none the wiser. The BOYS she had been warned about were now MEN. Working in her father's bait and tackle shop made it quite hard to avoid MEN, but her father was always there, keeping watch over her. After long, boring days hanging bags of freeze-dried bait (the buckets of live maggots were long gone), snagging her fingers on razor-sharp hooks and avoiding eye-contact with customers, she would go home alone, having moved out of her father's house at the first opportunity. Not because of any bad memories, or because she hated her father, she didn't. But because of the life-long suffocation she felt under his roof, like a knitted scarf wrapped too tightly around her neck, at once scratchy and restrictive but strangely comforting. It only lifted when she walked down by the river. One day, not long out of college and just shy of her nineteenth birthday, she saw the chance to escape. A tiny cottage, nestled into a bank overlooking the river with a For Rent sign outside.

Living on her own by the water, the mornings were the best, so quiet and still. Another night survived. No intruder, no burglar, no rapist bursting in through the window to attack her, no murderer in the dark. Her father told her she shouldn't live alone, it wasn't safe, but she did it anyway. Not out of spite, but just to prove to herself that she could. She was used to the solitary nights now, the creaks of her small, but perfectly formed house settling into its night-time routine.

Every Friday and Sunday she went to her father's for dinner. It was their routine, year in year out. In turn, her father visited her at least twice a week, but always unannounced, always on different days and at different times. He would enter her little two-up two-down, cramped as it was, with eyes everywhere, as if looking for something, some sign of a MANFRIEND. This made Juno laugh. Sometimes he would come straight out and ask her.

'Doing anything nice this weekend, Junie?' He always called her Junie.

'Just meeting a friend for lunch.'

'Is it a MANFRIEND?'

'No, Dad. It's Lucy, from school. Remember Lucy?'

Of course he remembered Lucy. Lucy was someone you couldn't forget.

Over their lunch date, Lucy proudly regaled Juno with her latest sexual escapades, drawing side-eyes and tuts from nearby diners. Loud Lucy with her frizzy hair and flicky eye-liner.

'Ssh, Lucy, everyone is staring at us,' Juno hissed as she tried to hide behind her menu.

'Oh fuck 'em, everyone has sex.'

She has no idea, thought Juno. She just thinks I'm a private person, not a frigid freak, a virgin at twenty-eight.

Lucy was still talking, she realised, so Juno tuned back in, just in case she was required to give some further input into the conversation.

'…I mean, can you imagine having the best orgasm of your life with someone you despise?'

'No,' Juno said, with total honesty. 'I cannot imagine that at all.'

Of course, she wasn't a stranger to the little death, but it was always death by her own hand. Juno could not see the point of having a man in her life, other than her father. She had redecorated her whole house many times in the years that she had lived there. She had tiled her bathroom, undertaken a basic plumbing course and even laid her own carpets. She heard her friends tell stories about how they would trap spiders under glasses for their boyfriends to dispose of when they got home. If Juno ever found a spider, she treated the spider the same way the spider treated her; with cautious indifference. You stay out of my way, I'll stay out of yours. Living on the riverbank, as she did, meant Juno had more wildlife to worry about than simple house-spiders. She followed the fortunes of a family of swans who nested on the opposite bank. One morning she had opened her door to find what appeared to be a damp ball of grey fluff deposited by her front gate. It turned out to be dazed swan chick, stolen from the nest and dropped by a fox. She nursed it back to health as best she could, making a bed of grass and damp rushes under a bush in her garden, finding worms for it to feed on. Then one day, it was gone. She always hoped he had made his own way back to his family. This was her river, her world. Why would she want to let a man into it and spoil everything?

Her father never told her she was special any more. What he did do was read weather reports, shipping forecasts, tidal graphs and fisheries bulletins. Nothing too unusual about this, his business depended on all of these things. But recently, Juno noticed he was becoming obsessed. Always telling her about rainfall variations in Belgium or pollution levels in the Sargasso Sea. He became so animated that Juno often had to tell him to calm down.

'But you don't understand, Junie. Changes in the North Atlantic Gyre could be devastating to marine life. Endangered species need to find a way to survive, whatever the cost, and we have to help them.'

'Never had you down as an eco-warrior, Dad.'

'There's a lot you don't know about me,' he replied, with a laugh that never reached his eyes.

April was bitter that year. The shallows of the river had a thin layer of ice, and a light sprinkle of snow even dusted the bare tops of the reed stems. Juno only had two fire-places to heat the whole house, so in the winter she slept under an electric blanket wearing bed-socks and thick pyjamas. It was unusual to need them come spring, but she was still waking up to her breath in clouds and frost on her windows. The swans were nesting, gathering rushes and sticks. She had read that the female swan was responsible for the building. Every now and then, the male would swoop down, his white wings spread wide, and drop off his latest find. Juno hoped the weather would improve before the eggs were laid. Could they survive such a cold?

Juno left the house early that morning, wrapped up in her thickest coat and scarf, to catch the young sun twinkling on the frost. She turned after locking her front door, to be confront by a shape crouched in the reed beds. Her heart thundered. A man. A MAN. A stranger so close to her sanctuary. But then he turned and smiled and seemed familiar somehow. He waved.

'It's Juno, isn't it?

She panicked. How did he know her name? What did he want? Was this what Father had been warning her about all along?

'Don't worry,' he said, sensing her fear. His accent was hard to place, but definitely not local. 'I know your father. When I told him where I would be working, he said I might find you here. My name is Guillaume.'

Juno's mouth remained closed, her feet rooted to the spot. In a flash of sudden blue and gold a kingfisher flapped its wings in take-off, making them both jump. They laughed in unison, and all at once, there was nothing scary about this man at all.

He was employed by the Environment Agency, he told her, undertaking a survey of native river populations, and had apparently visited her father's shop many times, which was why he looked familiar. Juno stopped listening after a while, not through boredom or rudeness, but because she found herself unable to concentrate on anything but his face. It was strange, not unpleasant, but not exactly handsome either. His skin was smooth, with a long, straight nose. His mouth seemed to come up to meet it, giving his face an almost pointed look. His lips were full and sensual. She wondered what it would be like to kiss them.

While he talked, Juno noticed a shifting inside her, somewhere undiscovered. Although he was telling her about commercial dams and underwater cameras, in her head, Juno heard him saying something entirely different.

'This is what we do,' he was whispering. 'Men and women. It's alright, I won't hurt you. This is what adults do. We talk, we make plans, we meet up and make sparks in damp caves, our bodies gliding over each in delicious ecstasy…'

'…isn't it?' His real voice cut off the sounds in Juno's head. She realised he had asked her a question while she was fantasising about this stranger. This MAN. She felt pathetic and embarrassed.

'You haven't been listening to a word I've been saying, have you?'

Juno cringed, waiting for the anger.

'I'm a nerd, I know it. I must be boring you to death. Why don't I buy you a coffee in town? I promise I won't talk about endangered species.'

Somehow, Juno heard herself say yes. She wanted to be where he was, this MAN, despite the wild pictures cavorting through her mind.

Somehow, later that night, she heard herself ask Guillaume back to her cottage. Her father's words echoed in her ears as she made drinks and got a fire going.

You're too special for BOYS.

There's a plan for you, you're special.

You don't need the attention of MEN.

But it felt so right. This was where she was meant to be. She had no idea what she was doing as she pulled her thick woolly jumper over her head and pulled him towards her on the sofa.

Other than the fire, the moonlight through the open curtains was the only illumination. She went to close them, but Guillaume stayed her hand.

'But what if someone sees,' she murmured.

'Who? The moon? The river? Let them watch.'

Let them watch, Juno thought, as her body slid over his, as his tongue slipped into her mouth, as her mouth sought out hidden places.

Let them watch.

The embers of the fire had died low when Juno woke up. Her nakedness, so exhilarating before, now left her feeling cold and exposed.

He was gone.

Of course he was gone.

She sat up, dragging the blanket from the back of the sofa and wrapping it around her shivering shoulders.

He had got what he wanted and left. All the chatting and laughing and coffee meant nothing.

He had gone.

She heard movement behind her, the creaking of a wooden chair.

She jumped up to see a shadow, sitting in the dark at her dining table.

'You scared me. I thought you'd gone,' Juno laughed, half through fear, half through relief.

He stayed silent.

'Shall I put the kettle on?' she asked, not knowing the correct etiquette for situations such as this.

'It's done then,' came the reply, in a voice that

made her legs turn to ice.

'What are you doing here?' She could barely speak. Could barely breathe.

'It doesn't matter,' he said, moving into the light. 'All that matters is, it's done. I can't say I'm happy, but this is the way it has to be. The way it always had to be.'

Her father slammed the door.

2. REBIRTH

Night-time in the reeds. She hears the frogs chirping and bulging. The August moon's gaze gently bathes her rounded belly. It has only been four months since that night, that distant, delicious, disgraceful night. That was another Juno, another body, not the one she inhabits now.

She can feel them inside her. She knows there is more than one. Twins? Triplets? Who can say, but she knows she should not be showing this much so early on.

It can only be Guillaume. There has been no-one else.

Juno thinks of her mother, how afraid she must have been. It already feels like the babies are going to split her in two and there are still months to go.

She only becomes whole at night, when her outer body and inner turmoil are finally joined. They are still in the dark, calmed. It is in the daylight that they frolic and flail inside her.

She has not visited a midwife.

Father must know, must see by now, but says nothing. He can barely look at her anymore. Strange people visit him in the shop most days, just as he is closing up and Juno is going home. She sees their eyes roving over her, over her body, as if checking for something, but they never look her in the eye.

Home is her only sanctuary.

So here she lies. Fat, full, waxing under her midwife moon. She feels at once utterly alone and connected to everyone and everything. Is this what motherhood is? This kinship with the world?

She massages oil into her stretched middle, while beneath her fingers the skin rolls and roils. Shapes come to the surface, then return to the deep like mythical sea-monsters. Is it a foot? An elbow? Something else? More join in. Two, three, five. She jolts her hand away and they stop. She pours the whole bottle of oil over her nakedness. She is slick, glistening, her stomach now still.

No-one is around as she leaves the cottage and slips into the midnight waters of the river. Juno wades slowly away from the bank. If someone should see me, she wonders to herself, what would they think?

She is a lunatic.

Ophelia on her lily-pad path.

All she knows is the water is safe, cool, nourishing.

Home.

Her feet leave the cushion of river grass and she floats, weightless. She lays back and watches the stars play out their eternal pantomime, for the stars are really suns, thousands, millions of suns, burning themselves into eventual oblivion.

But Juno only needs one moon.

As she closes her eyes, her other senses sharpen. She hears rustling from the bank. A fox perhaps? A swan? More noise. A light splash. Something is in the water with her.

Someone.

She struggles to right herself as her eyes flick open. Weeds tangle themselves around her wrists and ankles. Her stomach tightens, muscles contracting to become a solid rock that threatens to sink her. She smacks her hands on the surface, gulps down a mouthful of water and finally manages to stand. Pain zig-zags across her middle.

She sees eyes.

All around her, pale faces peer from the reeds. Some have even entered the water.

A figure wades towards her. She hasn't seen him in four months, but recognises Guillaume instantly. His hair is longer now, and slicked back from his forehead. He has a sheen all over, looking sleek and lithe as he cuts through the water, reaching out a hand to Juno.

'It is time,' he says, in his odd accent, and wraps his fingers around her wrist. His skin feels cold and slippery. Juno is utterly repulsed by this man. This creature. She thinks back to her friend Lucy's words. Imagine. Just imagine having the best orgasm of your life with someone you despise.

She tries to yank her arm away, but his grip is firm. Another jolt of pain hits. Her pelvic bone is on fire, the pressure building inside, pushing down her legs, muscles cramping and contracting.

'Let me go!' Juno screams in his face, but he just smiles, his mouth tight, snake-like.

'You must relax,' he coos. 'It is time. Here, let us help you.'

More bodies begin to join Guillaume and Juno in the water, faces she doesn't recognise blurring into one, all reaching out to her, to stroke her belly as if she is some swollen golden deity who can bestow a lifetime of good luck with her touch.

'Stop it! Get off, get off!' Juno shrieks, tears coming now. She tries swatting their hands away, but still more come, until she is totally surrounded by faces bearing down on her. She can no longer see the river bank or her cottage. She looks up, beyond the desperate, leering faces of those closing in on her, looks up into the black forever. She wishes that this would end, that these people would leave her alone, that she could go home.

As if in direct response to Juno's heavenly pleas, they all stop pawing and pressing against her and silently part. A thick cloud drifts in front of the moon. There is one final worshipper to join the throng.

'It's alright, Junie, just let it happen. It's time.

Then you can carry on with your life. But this needs to happen.'

Her father walks slowly towards her through the water until he is in up to his waist.

'I'm so sorry. I'm sorry we lost your mother. I'm sorry you had to be the one. I'm sorry the world is in such a mess that we needed you, my only daughter, to save us, to save them, but that's the way it must be. That's the way it has always been.'

His last few words are drowned out by Juno's screams as a violent contraction rips through her. She feels her bowels let go. She feels the need to evacuate, empty everything and push. An urge as primal as fighting for your last breath when your head is under water. Juno is unable to think, unable to do anything other than roar at the pain and push. She feels a rush between her legs. Not a baby, something else. Spools of liquid spaghetti pour from inside her, flickering over her submerged thighs, tickling the back of her knees.

'They are coming!' Guillaume shouts, to whoops of ecstatic delight.

Juno tries to reach down but her arms are being held fast. The pain subsides for a second, and she lifts her head, before another agonising strike hits her womb and she has to push again. Heat pulsates inside her, forcing its way out. There are more this time, Juno's screams drowning out the sound of thrashing and flailing in the water. With the inhuman strength that only the damned possess, she wrenches her wrists free and scoops up the bloody, frothing mess between her legs. Hundreds of clear, wriggling noodles spill from her hands, worms made of molten glass. She tries to stand, to run, but the pain takes her legs from under her.

'They are saved!' comes the exaltation from the throng still surrounding her. 'They are saved!'

Juno sees her father chanting along with them, reaching his hands to the sky, tears streaming down his face. Guillaume takes her arm, tenderly this time, and helps to get her balance.

'You did it!' he shouts in her face. 'We did it! We saved them.'

Drained of all energy, Juno can barely speak.

'Saved who? What are you talking about? What's happening to me?'

'I told you, right here by these reeds. Don't you remember?'

Through her agony and exhaustion, Juno tries to think back to that day. He had talked a lot about endangered native species, about how human kind was destroying their habitats and how things needed to change. He talked about how greed was killing the planet and about how sometimes sacrifices needed to be made. He talked about…

'Eels,' Juno whispers, the last vestiges of strength leaving her body. The water around her is no longer a gentle, lapping caress but a soup of horror. She can see them, ghostly shapes coiling and writhing around each other, around her. They are attracted to her, to the blood. Tiny pinpricks on her skin make her shiver. Unable to move, Juno pleads for help, begs to be set free.

'Dad? Please, I just want to sleep, help me.'

He starts to wade forward, his arms outstretched. His eyes are full of love, of devotion.

'Of course, my darling Junie, come on. You've done enough now, you deserve a rest.'

His fingers brush against hers, only to be slapped away by Guillaume.

'No. She stays.'

Her father yelps like a beaten dog and drops his eyes to the water, an act of deference, of respect.

'I have done everything you asked. I offered up my only daughter. She has played her part, we both have. Please, let us go.'

'But our children must feed.'

Guillaume nods to his followers and they take Juno's father by the arms, hoist him up above their heads, despite his kicks and pleas, and pass him down the line towards the bank. Juno sees his feet as they disappear behind the congregation, hears the thud as he hits the ground, feels the empty silence that follows, knowing he must have hit the ground skull first.

'Why?' Juno whimpers, pinpricks becoming razor slashes as more of the creatures latch onto her skin under the water.

'Why does the fox scavenge human detritus? Why does the vole devour its own young? Why does the electric eel shock? Survival.'

'Why me?'

'Juno,' he says, in a tone somehow both reverential and condescending, the way one would talk to a beloved child. 'It has always been you, daughter of the Snow Moon.'

His devotees have now turned their backs on her, wading their path towards the bank, back to their normal lives. Just as on that night four months ago, she has served her purpose. As the crowd disperses, she sees her father's body, his neck at a strange angle. She is glad she cannot she his face. If by some miracle he is still alive, she is glad he cannot see hers. Flooded with shame, Juno cannot help but float, unable to fight her maternal instincts. Guillaume was right. Her babies need to feed.

More tiny mouths, delicate and precise, drain her blood. Juno is lightheaded, her vision blurring. She sees Guillaume's triumphant face illuminated as the moon breaks free from the clouds. Oxytocin floods her brain and Juno feels that rush of love, the love her mother was only allowed for a few brief moments. She wraps her arms around her, cradling the baby eels to her naked breasts. The ones that are feeding on her thighs and buttocks begin to wriggle their way up her body, inchworms devouring everything they touch. Just as her eyes are closing, just as she is on the cusp of sacrificing herself entirely, a cacophony of white feathers and beady black eyes swoop down. Beating wings and pecking beaks descend upon Guillaume as he tries to run, his water-logged clothing dragging him down. The swans surround him, making no sound other than their powerful wings slapping the surface as they keep his head under the water. It is the last sound Juno hears before she blacks out.

Warm sun on her eyelids. The softness of feathers. The smell of the damp earth. Lightning flashes follow nerve paths in patterns across her breasts. They are full, aching.

She opens her eyes.

Juno is curled, bloodied, naked and foetus-like, in a nest of rushes. Behind the reeds, the river flows, forever changed but flowing still. But here she is safe. Here she is protected.

In the years that follow, she will think of her children often.

She hopes they made it to the sea.

FIRE ESCAPE

Come, walk the fire with me
Just for today
Slowly
Deliberately
Footstep by footstep
Bare skin on burning coal
Salamander
I cut off a limb
A new clutch of nerves exposed
Raw
Electric
Lightning trees
Spread their boughs
Needles and pins and knives and saw blades
And razor edged sharks teeth
Piercing through muscle and bone
Leg in a bear trap
Arm in a sling
Fingers are tingling
Pain fibres sing
I only have so many spoons
I sleep under tramadol moons
When walking and sitting
And talking
Is exhausting
I do not get better

I do not get well
No remission
No respite
No release from this Hell
Proceed calmly to the exit
There is only one way out
Of what they call
The Suicide Disease

ABOUT THE AUTHOR

Em Dehaney is a mother of two, a writer of fantasy and a drinker of tea. Born in Gravesend, England, her writing is inspired by the history of her home town. She is made of tea, cake, blood and magic. By night she is editor and whip-cracker at Burdizzo Books. By day you can always find her at **http://www.emdehaney.com/** or lurking about on Facebook posting pictures of witches **https://www.facebook.com/emdehaney/**

Her main literary influences are Stephen King, Neil Gaiman, Graham Masterton, Angela Carter and the Poppy Z Brite books by Billy Martin, and while her published works to date have been mostly horror, Em writes anything that takes her fancy and doesn't like to be pinned down to one genre. A lifelong music lover, Em will listen to everything from acid house to experimental jazz, but her main musical inspiration often comes from Bjork, Fiona Apple, Regina Spektor, PJ Harvey and Super Furry Animals. Her obsessions include reading about Jack The Ripper, Reese's Peanut Butter Cups and smashing the patriarchy.

BRAVE BOY
BOOKS

Printed in Great Britain
by Amazon

85830219R00079